Praise for
The Who & The What

"Disarmingly funny. A fiery...probing new play, crackling with ideas."   —Charles Isherwood, *New York Times*

"Vibrant. Strong and colorful. A culture-clash drama simmering with humor."   —Associated Press

"Fearless...powerful...Ayad Akhtar is...prodigiously talented."
                                    —Jeremy Gerard, *Deadline*

"Continually absorbing...Akhtar has a splendid command of structure, and...a fine ear for dialogue."   —*The New Yorker*

"Funny and insightful. A blistering rebuke of a traditionalist, unquestioning view of Islam."
                                —Zachary Stewart, *Theatermania*

"Akhtar is a provocative, wise and funny playwright."
                                —Steven Suskin, *Huffington Post*

Praise for
Disgraced

"The best play I saw last year....A quick-witted and shattering drama.... *Disgraced* rubs all kinds of unexpected raw spots with intelligence and humor." —Linda Winer, *Newsday*

"A sparkling and combustible contemporary drama....Ayad Akhtar's one-act play deftly mixes the political and personal, exploring race, freedom of speech, political correctness, even the essence of Islam and Judaism. The insidery references to the Hamptons and Bucks County, Pennsylvania, and art critic Jerry Saltz are just enough to make audience members feel smart.... Akhtar...has lots to say about America and the world today. He says it all compellingly, and none of it is comforting."
—Philip Boroff, *Bloomberg Businessweek*

"Compelling.... *Disgraced* raises and toys with provocative and nuanced ideas." —Jesse Oxfeld, *New York Observer*

"A continuously engaging, vitally engaged play about thorny questions of identity and religion in the contemporary world....In dialogue that bristles with wit and intelligence, Mr. Akhtar...puts contemporary attitudes toward religion under a microscope, revealing how tenuous self-image can be for people born into one way of being who have embraced another....Everyone has been told that politics and religion are two subjects that should be off-limits at social gatherings. But watching Mr. Akhtar's characters rip into these forbidden topics, there's no arguing that they make for ear-tickling good theater." —Charles Isherwood, *New York Times*

"Ninety minutes of sharp contemporary theatre at its argumentative, and disturbing, best." —Robert McCrum, *The Guardian*

"*Disgraced* stands among recent marks of an increasing and welcome phenomenon: the arrival of South Asian and Middle Eastern Americans as presences in our theater's dramatis personae, matching their presence in our daily life. Like all such phenomena, it carries a double significance. An achievement and a sign of recognition for those it represents, for the rest of us it constitutes the theatrical equivalent of getting to know the new neighbors—something we had better do if we plan to survive as a civil society." —Michael Feingold, *Village Voice*

"It's a rare work that jolts an audience into cries of pained shock, but Ayad Akhtar's Pulitzer-winner...does just that. A powerful, challenging, deftly crafted work, this is a bold exploration of race, culture and what it means to be Muslim in post-9/11 America....A clever, gripping modern American tragedy." —*Sunday Times*

The Who &
The What

ALSO BY AYAD AKHTAR

Disgraced
American Dervish

The Who & The What

A PLAY

AYAD AKHTAR

BACK BAY BOOKS
Little, Brown and Company
New York Boston London

Back Bay Books / Little, Brown and Company
Hachette Book Group
1290 Avenue of the Americas, New York, NY 10104
littlebrown.com

First edition: October 2014

Back Bay Books is an imprint of Little, Brown and Company. The Back Bay Books name and logo are trademarks of Hachette Book Group, Inc.

The publisher is not responsible for websites (or their content) that are not owned by the publisher.

The Hachette Speakers Bureau provides a wide range of authors for speaking events. To find out more, go to hachettespeakersbureau.com or call (866) 376-6591.

ISBN 978-0-316-32449-6
LCCN 2014948354

10 9 8 7 6 5 4 3 2

LSC-H

Printed in the United States of America

For my father. For Kimberly. And for Bernie.

AUTHOR'S NOTE

Whereas tragedies are stories of subtraction, comedies depict a process of addition. In a tragedy there are fewer characters at the end of the story than at its beginning. *All My Sons, Death of a Salesman, A View from the Bridge,* all end with the passing of protagonists. At the close of *Hamlet*'s final act, the court at Elsinore is ravaged by elimination. And even when death is not a literal end, the tragic sense speaks to us of life's inevitable loss.

Comedy, as tragedy's opposite number, offers a depiction of life in the key of hope. This is why comedies so often end with marriage, a fulfillment that is more than a trope, an image of union and continuity, the archetypal precondition for the promise of new life.

It may seem strange to some for a play about the place of women in Islam to end comedically. For what, indeed, is funny about the troubling gender politics that obtain in so many quarters of the Muslim world? These would perhaps be the rightful subject of biting satire but certainly not of heartfelt comedy. But that is exactly what I hoped to bring off with *The Who & The What*.

I started this play as a dialogue with another comedy. The Bard's *Taming of the Shrew* had always beguiled me, driven by a tension that seemed obsolete to the plights of modern men and women but speaking eloquently to my own experience of gender relations as a Pakistani American. One evening, in a New York cab, I reencountered *Shrew* in the form of an ad for *Kiss Me, Kate*. It was the spark that ignited the kindling I had been gathering for years. I had long been circling around the idea of a story in which a bright young Pakistani American woman attempts to separate from her father, with her deep filial piety, the circumstance of her mother's death, and her own existential anxieties all working against her. She has found a way to proceed with the inner work incumbent on anyone wishing to individuate, but only by channeling her defiance, longing, and outrage into the writing of a book.

That book is no laughing matter: She is penning a humanizing, historically revisionist novel depicting an episode from the Prophet's life, the circumstances around the so-called revelation of the veil. Her procedure is literary, but her challenge is something more than artistic. For her father's religious devotion is part of the yoke she must throw off. Her book is, among other things, her instrument of rebellion.

For some time I had been preoccupied with the Prophet as a literary figure, his representation a construction that mirrored tropes from the Old and New Testaments. But any challenge to the received portrait we Muslims have of the Prophet is certainly not yet as primary a matter as the conflict that the challenge itself represents, a conflict familiar to us from the Rushdie affair and other similar controversies, and hardly the subject of comedy.

And yet, my long-standing preoccupation with the representation of the Prophet only came alive for me with the promise of a story about it rendered, as comedy is, in the key of hope. I have often felt that any good narrative idea is actually a convergence of three or four ideas, and in this case one of them was — decidedly — the notion of a story of addition, not subtraction.

So were these characters born and, as characters tend to do, they proved to have their own intentions. And yet, through their many unexpected reversals and revelations, one thing was constant: an abiding love between them that kept this story on comedic footing even as it turned darker and more unforgiving. A story about addition, then, but never without subtraction on its mind, one that completes with the comedic trope of a baby, but a baby whose arrival only seems to promise further dissonance ahead.

Perhaps this is as it must be, a tension embodying and expressing the inevitable loss that even the most redeeming act of self-creation occasions. Indeed, one of the perplexities of writing this play was the long process of coming to understand the fight at the heart of it: not just that of a daughter with her father, but that of my love for and my battle with my heritage, my family, my tradition.

Can we belong and yet be separate? Is the process of individuation fundamentally one of loss or gain? These are the questions the play is asking, and its comedic form more than hints at a response. For indeed, art seldom provides anything like answers, and yet, sometimes *form* is answer enough.

Ayad Akhtar
Los Angeles
June 2014

PRODUCTION
HISTORY

The Who & The What had its world premiere on February 19, 2014, at La Jolla Playhouse in La Jolla, California (Christopher Ashley, artistic director; Michael S. Rosenberg, managing director). It was directed by Kimberly Senior; the set design was by Jack Magaw; the costume design was by Elisa Benzoni; the lighting design was by Jaymi Lee Smith; the sound design was by Jill BC Du Boff; and the stage manager was Dana DePaul. The cast was as follows:

ZARINA...Monika Jolly
MAHWISH...Meera Rohit Kumbhani
AFZAL...Bernard White
ELI...Kai Lennox

The Who & The What received its New York premiere at LCT3 / Lincoln Center Theater (André Bishop, artistic director; Paige Evans, artistic director/LCT3; Adam Siegel, managing director) on June 16, 2014. It was directed by Kimberly Senior; the set design was by Jack Magaw; the costume design was by Emily Rebholz; the lighting design was by Japhy Weideman; the sound design was by Jill BC Du Boff; the stage manager was Megan Schwarz Dickert. The cast was as follows:

ZARINA...Nadine Malouf
MAHWISH...Tala Ashe
AFZAL...Bernard White
ELI...Greg Keller

The Who &
The What

Gentlemen, importune me no farther,

For how I firmly am resolv'd you know:

That is, not to bestow my youngest daughter

Before I have a husband for the elder.

—*The Taming of the Shrew*, Act 1, Sc. 1

Act One: Scene One

Present day. Atlanta, Georgia.

A kitchen. In it:

Zarina—32, of South Asian origin—gimlet-gazed, lovely, though her appearance already lightly worn from worry. And...

Her younger sister, Mahwish—25—light and carefree. Even lovelier. A real knockout.

Both are American-born; both speak without any accent.

Zarina is in an apron, chopping vegetables.

MAHWISH: Stop changing the subject.

ZARINA: There was a subject?

MAHWISH: Zarina, did you get that link I sent you or not?

ZARINA: Wish. There is no universe. In which I start. Online dating.

MAHWISH: Z...if you don't start showing *some* interest, Dad is not gonna let me—

ZARINA (*Cutting her off*): You don't need me to get married for you and Haroon to get married.

Beat.

MAHWISH: You're just *flouting* Dad.

ZARINA: *Flouting?*

MAHWISH: Because you can.

ZARINA: Do you even know what that word means?

MAHWISH: Yes, I know what it means. And I know it comes from a Dutch word that means to hiss at. In derision—

ZARINA *(Impressed, lightly sarcastic)*: Wow.

MAHWISH *(Over)*: Manuel says learning the words isn't enough. You have to learn where they come from.

ZARINA: Manuel. Your GRE teacher.

MAHWISH: Yeah?

ZARINA: With the muscles and the tank top.

MAHWISH: So Manuel's a stud? What does that have to do with—

ZARINA: Does Haroon know how you feel about Manuel?

MAHWISH: I don't *feel* anything. I just think he's hot—

ZARINA: I think it's good. You're acknowledging your desire for someone other than Haroon.

MAHWISH *(Over)*: I'm not *acknowledging* desire. I don't have any *desire* for Manuel.

ZARINA *(Lightly taunting)*: Manuel. Manuel.

MAHWISH: You're just trying to change the subject again...
I can't get married before you do, Zarina.

ZARINA: That's absurd. This is not Pakistan.

MAHWISH: It's not what's done.

ZARINA: Neither is having anal sex with your prospective husband so that you can prove to his parents you're a virgin when you finally marry him.

MAHWISH: I can't believe you just—

ZARINA: There has to be a better solution. Prick your finger. Bleed on the sheet—

MAHWISH: You're disgusting.

ZARINA: You're the one doing it.

MAHWISH: Here's what I know about you. Anything I tell you, sooner or later, you will use against me.

ZARINA: I'm a Scorpio.

MAHWISH: It's a character failing.

ZARINA: Shoot me.

MAHWISH *(Suddenly)*: Why are you cutting an avocado?

ZARINA: For the salad?

MAHWISH: We hate avocados.

ZARINA: *You* hate avocados.

MAHWISH: *Dad* hates avocados.

ZARINA: I love them.

MAHWISH: See? Flouting.

   (Pause)

   I never told you this…

   You know that book you have of the Prophet's sayings about sex. On your shelf…

ZARINA: Yeah?

MAHWISH: One day I was in your room and, when I saw it there, I had this weird feeling like I should take it down and open it. So I did. You know what I opened to? The Prophet saying that wives are like farms. That husbands could farm them any way they wanted. From the front or back. But not in the anus.

ZARINA: So the sin is on the farmer. Not the farm.

MAHWISH: Really?

ZARINA: Wish, I don't think any of us should be taking sex advice from the Prophet.

MAHWISH: Then why do you have the book?

7

ZARINA: If you're so worried, stop doing it.

MAHWISH: He's a man. If I don't do something with him, he'll find somebody else to do it with…

(Beat)

So you don't think I'm gonna go to *dozakh?*

ZARINA: Wish, you know I don't believe in hell.

MAHWISH: But what if you're wrong? Manuel said there was this philosopher guy—

ZARINA: You and Manuel were talking about a *philosopher?*

MAHWISH: This guy named Pasta.

ZARINA: Pasta?

MAHWISH: Who said that he wasn't sure if there was a hell but it was better to believe in one just in case.

ZARINA: Pascal.

MAHWISH: Okay. Whatever.

ZARINA: And that's not actually what Pascal said.

MAHWISH: How are you not scared of hell?

ZARINA: I can't be scared of something I don't believe in.

MAHWISH: It's in the Quran.

ZARINA: It's a metaphor.

MAHWISH: For what?

ZARINA: For suffering. For the cycle of human suffering.

Mahwish considers her sister. Impressed.

MAHWISH: See…you're so smart. You're beautiful. You're young. But you behave…like a…hurr*id*ian.

ZARINA: A what?

MAHWISH: You know…a bossy old woman.

ZARINA (*Pronouncing it correctly*): Harridan?

MAHWISH: Is that how you say it?

ZARINA: *Harridan.* Repeat after me. *Harridan*—

MAHWISH: You're like one of those compound wives on *Big Love.*

ZARINA: What in God's name are you talking—

MAHWISH *(Continuing)*: Too bad they canceled it. You'd be perfect. Married to me and Dad. I feel like you're my sister wife.

ZARINA: You're truly insane.

MAHWISH: Dutiful. Despotic.

ZARINA: That was right.

MAHWISH: Thank you. Up and at 'em at six thirty. Cooking breakfast.

ZARINA: For you and Dad.

MAHWISH: I never asked you to cook me breakfast.

ZARINA: You're an ungrateful brat.

MAHWISH: You wanna cook breakfast? You wanna clean? Fine. I'm just saying, there's better things for you to be doing.

ZARINA: Like cooking and cleaning and having babies with someone I don't love?

MAHWISH: I love Haroon.

ZARINA: I know you do.

Mahwish's phone sounds with a text. She checks.

MAHWISH: Some new barista at Java on the Park recognized Dad from TV. Gave him a free cappuccino.
(Off another text, reading, perplexed)
The eagle has landed.

ZARINA: The what?

Another text.

MAHWISH (CONT'D): God.

ZARINA: What now?

Mahwish shows the text to Zarina.

ZARINA (CONT'D): Dad's sticking his tongue out at you?

MAHWISH: He just discovered emoticons. It's so annoying.
(*Typing into phone*)
Busy.
(*Beat*)
You won't go online dating. You won't let me set you up
with Yasmeen's brother —

ZARINA (CONT'D): My life is fine. Leaves me time and space to
write.

MAHWISH: So you keep saying.

ZARINA: What is that supposed to mean?

MAHWISH: You never talk about what you're writing. You never
show anybody anything —

ZARINA: Doesn't mean I don't write —

MAHWISH: Why don't you ever talk about it?

ZARINA: Because I don't want to.

MAHWISH: So you actually write when you go to the library?
'Cause that's not what the librarian said.

ZARINA: What librarian?

MAHWISH: The blonde. Stacy. She's in my yoga class. She says
you stare out the window for hours.

ZARINA: I've had writer's block. That's why I've been staring out
the window.
(*Beat*)
And I don't just stare out the window. Sometimes I
masturbate.

MAHWISH: You what?

ZARINA: Stacy didn't tell you that?

MAHWISH: In public?

ZARINA: The desk I sit at is in the corner.

MAHWISH *(Intrigued)*: What's the book about?

ZARINA: This really hot guy who teaches me amazing words in my GRE class. It's called *Manuel*.

Beat.

MAHWISH: Why can't you just tell me what it's about?

ZARINA: Gender politics.

MAHWISH: Hello? English?

ZARINA: Women and Islam.

Beat.

MAHWISH: Like what, like bad stuff?

ZARINA: Not only.

MAHWISH: Well, I hope not. 'Cause everyone's always making a big deal about women in Islam. We're just fine.

ZARINA: Good to know.

MAHWISH: You don't actually do that in the library, do you?

ZARINA: For me to know, and you and Stacy to find out...

Pause.

MAHWISH: You're hiding, Z. Behind the cooking and the cleaning and the "I'm working on gender politics..."
(Beat)
You have to put Ryan behind you.

Pause.

ZARINA: He is.

MAHWISH: No, he's not.
>	(Beat)
>>	He's married—
ZARINA (*Cutting her off*): I know!

Zarina is suddenly emotional.

MAHWISH: I didn't want to tell you...
>	I found him on Facebook...
>	He's with his wife and they're holding a baby.

Zarina is clearly affected at hearing this.

Mahwish goes to comfort her.

Zarina walks out.

Act One: Scene Two

A bench. At Java on the Park.

On it: a South Asian man—60—in a Georgia Tech Yellow Jackets sweatshirt—on his smartphone as he sips coffee.

This is Afzal, Zarina and Mahwish's gregarious, larger-than-life father. He has a very noticeable Indo-Pak accent.

Afzal looking at his phone…

AFZAL: C'mon, Mahwish. I know you got my text. It says read at twelve thirty-one.

Just as Eli—30—enters. White, with a beard, looking cleaned up and eager. Not particularly handsome, but very soulful.

Afzal notices him. Types into his phone…

AFZAL (CONT'D) (_Quietly_): The eagle has landed.
(_Putting down his phone, standing_)
   Eli?
ELI (_Surprised_): Yes?
AFZAL (_Going to shake hands_): Afzal, Afzal Jatt.
ELI: Do I know you?
AFZAL: Zarina's father.

ELI: Her father?

AFZAL: She didn't tell you?

ELI: Tell me what?

AFZAL: We thought it best you met with me first.

ELI: Oh.

AFZAL: Young man, we are a conservative family. She just thought—
I just thought...

ELI: Uh-huh.

AFZAL: You're disappointed.

ELI *(Evasive)*: No, no, no...I just don't know why she didn't let
me know...

AFZAL: Would you have come?

ELI: I mean...

AFZAL: And I wasn't going to let her meet you face-to-face without me meeting you first...So you see...it really couldn't be
any other way.

ELI: Couldn't it?

AFZAL: You'd be surprised at the types you meet *online,* young
man.

    (Off Eli's continued perplexity)

    Take a seat. Can I get you something?

ELI: Uh—

AFZAL *(Winning)*: C'mon, take a seat. You came this far. Might
as well...

    You drink coffee? You like coffee?

ELI: Sure.

AFZAL: Milk? Sugar?

ELI: Black.

AFZAL: Drinks it like a man. I love it.

Afzal exits.

Eli looks around, uncomfortable.

Beat.

Afzal's phone sounds with a text.

Another beat.

Afzal returns, a cup of coffee in hand.

AFZAL (CONT'D): Dark roast.

ELI: What do I owe you?

AFZAL: On me. Actually, on the house. They recognized me from television…

ELI: Wait…you're…

AFZAL: *Always there for you.*

ELI: The taxi company.

AFZAL: Zama Yellow Cab.

ELI: Right. Zama.

AFZAL: Named after my two girls. Za-rina, Ma-hwish. Zama.

ELI: 444-ZAMA?

AFZAL: Do you have any idea how many hundreds of thousands of dollars it's taken to have that *jingle* printed on your brain?

ELI: Probably don't want to know, do I?

AFZAL: Why not?

ELI *(Pointing at Afzal's phone)*: You got a text…

Afzal picks up his phone. Checks.

Grunting to himself. Displeased.

AFZAL: Busy. Busy doing what, for God's sake? Busy ignoring your father.

ELI: Is that Zarina?

AFZAL *(Dismissive)*: No. The other one.

(Putting the phone down)

So—tell me about yourself, Eli.

ELI: So is she not coming?

AFZAL: No.

ELI: Um—you know, sir…I—uh—thanks for the coffee. I understand that you would want to know more about your daughter's potential romantic interest, but…I've never gone on a date with someone's *father* before.

AFZAL: Look. I told you. We're a conservative family. Humor me. Good news is: I like you already. Dignified. Restrained. Intelligent.

ELI: You can tell all that?

AFZAL: A man of my instincts, son. I've gone from driving a cab to owning thirty percent of the taxis in our great city. I know a winner when I see one.

C'mon.

(Beat)

So, you run a mosque in Cobb County.

ELI: How did you know?

Beat.

AFZAL: She told me.

ELI: What else did she tell you?

AFZAL: That you were a convert.

ELI: When I was twenty-three.

AFZAL: *Mashallah.* How did it happen?

ELI: Kind of a long story, sir…

AFZAL: You're my only appointment this afternoon.

Beat.

ELI: I grew up in Detroit, in the inner city. I've been around Islam as long as I can remember. First time I ever went to a mosque, I was in high school. I'd never experienced anything like it—

AFZAL: *Subhanallah.*

ELI: The sense of community. The call to prayer. Watching folks praying? It just—it opened me up. I wanted to be a part of that.

AFZAL: *Mashallah.* Being born into our faith is a great blessing. But even greater to find your way to it.

ELI: I don't think of it that way, sir. God's mercy belongs to everyone.

Afzal grunts.

AFZAL: So, what's this about a soup kitchen?

Beat.

ELI: Well, a lot of our folks eat pretty much one meal a day, and it's at our *masjid.* It's a pretty run-down part of town. We do a lot of home improvement. I'm a licensed plumber, actually.

AFZAL: Fix their houses. Then convert them. Good business plan.

ELI: Our outreach is more about serving others than bringing people to the faith.

AFZAL: You're a do-gooder!—

ELI: Well…

AFZAL: —Only good thing I did in my life, young man, is my two girls. They are the sum achievement of an otherwise

17

cosmically useless existence. Useless. Shuttling people back and forth. Half the time because they're too drunk to drive. Look. Don't get me wrong. Gotta put food on the table. Have to take care of my angels.

(Beat)

How much money do you make?

ELI: Excuse me?

AFZAL: You're not deaf, are you?

ELI: No, I'm not, sir.

AFZAL: So how much money do you make?

ELI: It's just...

AFZAL: What?

ELI: It's a personal question.

AFZAL: I'm assuming you have matrimonial intentions...

ELI: Matrimonial—

AFZAL: You listed "interested in marriage" on your online profile.

ELI: Look. I think your daughter is amazing...

AFZAL: You think my daughter is amazing? How would you know? From a profile? Pictures? Smiley faces?

ELI: Well, I've met her, actually.

AFZAL: You met her? Where? When?

ELI: About a year ago. At a talk at Georgia Tech. An event. With Ayaan Hirsi Ali.

AFZAL: That black woman?

ELI: Uh, yes, sir. She's black. She's from Somalia.

AFZAL: The one who thinks all Muslims should become Christian?

ELI: That's not exactly what she thinks—

AFZAL: Why would you go to that?!

ELI: I don't agree with everything she says—

AFZAL: She wants us to go running around confused, like Christians!

ELI: Confused?

AFZAL: Young man, Jesus Christ was a very good man, very important, we know that—Quran is very clear about that—but he was not the son of God.

ELI: Right.

AFZAL: What did Zarina think about this...*event?*

ELI: I'm not sure. We didn't speak about it that much. We ended up sitting next to each other. She seemed pretty engaged to me—

AFZAL *(Suddenly)*: Listen to me, young man. My daughter is a good Muslim. She has fifteen biographies of the Prophet Muhammad, peace be upon him. Fifteen! All lined up in her bedroom.

ELI: I don't doubt it, sir.

Afzal grunts.

AFZAL: So you spoke to her...then what?

ELI: That was it.

AFZAL: No telephone number? No text messaging?

ELI: I didn't get a chance to ask her...

But then, lo and behold, I saw her online...

AFZAL *(Sarcastic)*: A year later.

ELI: Yeah.

Beat.

AFZAL: You didn't say anything about this to me, Eli.

ELI: Say anything to *you?*

AFZAL *(Catching his own slip)*: To *her.* I mean, *she* didn't say anything to *me* about—

ELI *(Realizing something is amiss)*: Well...I wasn't exactly sure if it was her.

AFZAL: I don't know.

ELI: I figured I'd mention it when I saw her...

Beat. As Eli continues to sort through his confusion.

AFZAL: I liked you, Eli. I really did.

Beat.

ELI: Wait, are you leaving?

AFZAL *(Suddenly)*: Are you a pervert?

ELI: Excuse me?

AFZAL: I'm not going to find some wall in your bedroom covered with pictures of my daughter on it.

ELI: Whoa. Of course not.

AFZAL *(Over)*: Because if it's there, I will find it. I will.

ELI: I don't doubt that, sir.

Beat.

AFZAL: How much money do you make?

Act One: Scene Three

At home.

Zarina and Afzal. Arguing.

ZARINA: You did what?

AFZAL: It's not that big a deal, behti.

ZARINA: How many times have you done this?

AFZAL: Twice.

(Beat)

Okay...more than twice.

ZARINA: How many times?

AFZAL: I've been doing it a couple of months.

ZARINA: How many guys have you met?

AFZAL: Five.

ZARINA: For the love of God!

AFZAL: Now wait a second. Just hear me out—

ZARINA (Underneath): I don't believe this.

AFZAL: —He's a good man. He's intelligent. He's someone who can understand you.

ZARINA: Do you have any idea how inappropriate this is?

AFZAL: A year from now, if you're married to him, you'll look back on this—

ZARINA: If we're married? Dad. What are you talking about? Are you insane?

AFZAL: Just meet him.

ZARINA: No.

AFZAL: Please.

ZARINA: I am not having this discussion with you.

AFZAL: Zarina, behti. Listen to me. I met seven other young men—

ZARINA: So it was seven?

AFZAL: —all of them good-looking chaps, well employed, perfect son-in-laws...

ZARINA: Unbelievable.

AFZAL: I didn't come to you—

ZARINA: You opened an account in my name.

AFZAL: I didn't even try. Why not?

ZARINA *(Continuing)*: You posted pictures. You wrote messages pretending to be me.

AFZAL: —Because I knew. They were not right. You could not be happy with any of them. None of them would ever understand you. This one's different.

ZARINA: You're a piece of work!

AFZAL: You should be impressed I pulled it off.

ZARINA: Dad!

AFZAL: Behti, meet him.

ZARINA: No!

Pause.

AFZAL: He says he knows you.

THE WHO & THE WHAT

ZARINA: What?

AFZAL: He says he met you before. At a talk at Georgia Tech. That black woman.

ZARINA: Ayaan Hirsi Ali.

AFZAL: Who should be shot, by the way.

ZARINA: Stop it, Dad.

AFZAL: What do you see in her?

ZARINA: We're not getting into this.

AFZAL: You know she thinks Muslims should all convert to Christianity?

ZARINA: Well, I see her point.

AFZAL *(Stunned)*: What point?

ZARINA: She's just saying Christianity has been around longer than we have. It's had more time to work out some of the kinks.

AFZAL *(Snickering)*: Believing God can have a son is a sign of working out kinks?

ZARINA: I'm not talking about this with you—

AFZAL: You know what the Prophet said—

ZARINA: I know what the Prophet said—

AFZAL: Then why are you defending them?

ZARINA: Who?

AFZAL: Christians?

ZARINA: I'm not.

AFZAL *(Sarcastic)*: Son of God. As if God could have a son.

ZARINA: Well, if he's God he can do anything, right?

AFZAL: This is God we're talking about. Not some guest on David Letterman.

ZARINA: So...random.

(Beat)

So this guy you met…He said he knew me from the Hirsi Ali talk?

AFZAL: He says you had a nice conversation.

ZARINA *(Thinking)*: He's not white, is he?

AFZAL: Yes.

ZARINA: Glasses?

AFZAL: That's right.

ZARINA: What was his name again?

AFZAL: Eli.

ZARINA: Right. Eli.

(Beat)

He's a convert—

AFZAL: Quite a tale. You know he runs a soup kitchen and a *masjid* on the Northside?

ZARINA: I remember now.

AFZAL: Making people's lives better. He said he wanted to ask for your number, but he was too nervous. He was too impressed by you.

ZARINA: And what? He just saw me online?

AFZAL: Muslimlove.com. Your profile is amazing, behti. Your old father is not such a fool after all.

ZARINA: I never said you were a fool.

AFZAL: You don't go from driving a cab—

ZARINA *(Coming in, mimicking)*: To owning thirty percent of the taxis in Atlanta.

AFZAL: Don't make fun of me.

ZARINA: I'm not.

AFZAL: You are.

(Beat)

All I care about is the two of you. Your happiness. Why do you think I've busted my butt out there for thirty-five years? To make sure the three of you were taken care of. There's only two of you left. After that goddamn cancer took your mother.

ZARINA *(Off Afzal's sudden emotion)*: Dad, don't.

AFZAL: The point is, at least you and your sister are taken care of. You and your future families. Many times over—

ZARINA: I know, Dad.

AFZAL: You wouldn't have the freedom to be writing a book—

ZARINA: Dad. I know.

AFZAL: —and I encouraged it. When you got into Harvard, it was the proudest moment of my life. You wanted to study literature, philosophy? I encouraged it. You wanted to get an MFA in creative writing?

ZARINA: I know, I know...

AFZAL: You were the one who made me see that it's important we don't all become doctors and lawyers and whatnot. We need *our own kind* thinking about the bigger questions. But it takes money. Money, money, money. And it has to come from somewhere.

ZARINA: I know!

Beat.

AFZAL: You're not happy. You think I don't see that?

ZARINA: If I'm not happy it's because I haven't been able to write for months.

Pause.

25

AFZAL: Zarina. I'm sorry. I should not have stopped you and Ryan.

> Forgive me.

ZARINA: I have.

AFZAL: No you haven't.

Pause.

ZARINA: I didn't have to listen to you.

AFZAL: That you did says something about who you are.

ZARINA: I don't know that I like what it says.

AFZAL: I do.

Beat.

ZARINA: The kids were not going to be brought up Christian, Dad.

AFZAL: I know.

ZARINA: He'd agreed.

AFZAL: I know, behti.

Pause.

ZARINA *(Emotional)*: I'm not sure I know what love is anymore, Dad.

Another pause.

AFZAL: Zarina...

> Your mother, bless her soul—she was a saint...—I met that woman and the first thing I thought was, I don't like her. I just don't like her voice. I don't like her nose. I

don't like her. But that didn't matter. My father told me, That's your wife, that's the woman you'll marry, and there it was.

ZARINA: What was wrong with her nose?

AFZAL: Nothing, behti. Nothing.

ZARINA: I have her nose.

AFZAL: I was an idiot.

You know what? I fell in love with that nose! It turned out to be the perfect shape.

My nose against her nose? A classic! And her voice?

That was the voice of my soul.

I grew to love it more than Mehdi Hassan's.

ZARINA (Sarcastic): I'm sure Mom would be happy to hear that. "I loved you more than a has-been crooner…"

AFZAL: Mehdi Hassan was the bloody Frank Sinatra of Pakistan.

He was not a has-been crooner…—I was too soft on you, Zarina.

ZARINA: Here we go.

AFZAL: You should have more respect for your old father—

ZARINA: Dad. I was kidding—

AFZAL: Here I am trying to tell you something important—

ZARINA: Okay, Dad.

AFZAL (Continuing): I'm trying to tell you what happened to me.

Your mother was a gift, but I didn't see it. For three years I didn't see it!

Can you imagine that? Who would think you could wait three years in a marriage before finding love? Hmm? In this country? *I fell in love. I am so in love.* Here, when things start between two people, the water is already boiling. All it can do is cool off. Like your mother used to say, in the East, we start with a cold kettle, so it has room to heat up over the years.

(Beat)

You're old enough to know, behti—we lacked for nothing in the bedroom.

ZARINA: Dad.

AFZAL: It was not an instant chemistry...but when we found our rhythm, we *found* our rhythm.

ZARINA: Dad.

AFZAL: Your mother was an adventurous woman.

ZARINA: I don't need to...

AFZAL: I lacked for nothing.

ZARINA: I got it.

(Beat)

Why are you telling me this?

AFZAL: Context, Zarina. Context. I want you to understand the context of my choices.

If I made a mistake with you and Ryan it was because I had a different experience of love. My marriage was arranged. And it took time. *Time.* It was the only path to love I trusted.

(Beat)

Stop punishing yourself. Move on.

(Beat)

Meet the boy. Just meet him. If for no other reason, just to say to yourself: I. Am. Moving. On.

(Beat)

Meet him for your poor old father.

ZARINA: You're not poor. And you're not old.

AFZAL: For your lying and manipulative father.

Who only loves you. And who would gladly give his heart and his life for you to be happy.

Zarina considers him. Beat.

Act One: Scene Four

A restaurant.

Zarina and Eli. Talking.

ELI: So I grew up in a pretty committed house. Not religious denominationally...but committed, to changing things. Making people's lives better. I feel like they were getting away from their own pasts. My mom was a blue blood WASP from New England. She married a man from a Southern evangelical family. He was brought up that way, but he was an atheist. My dad, I mean.

ZARINA: I got that.

ELI: Obviously, sorry...

(Beat)

Anyway, Marx was the real prophet in our house.

I suppose the whole Freudian thing would be...I had to find a faith to piss my folks off and define myself and whatnot.

ZARINA: That's not really the whole Freudian thing.

ELI: It isn't?

ZARINA: The Freudian thing would be more like: If your mother secretly harbored devotional tendencies and hid them from your father, who, as the Marxist, would have thought religion was for fools...

ELI: Which he did.

ZARINA *(Continuing)*: And if, say, you and your mother bonded over talk about religion because that was what she could never discuss with your father, her husband—

ELI: Right...

ZARINA: —If that were the case...then your choice of a religious life would be a challenge to your father's authority, while bringing you closer to your mother in a secret way he could never compete with.

ELI: Huh...

ZARINA: In essence, you would have found a way—metaphorically speaking—to have married your mother and killed your father. Without, of course, realizing that you did it. Just like Oedipus.

ELI: That's pretty much it.

ZARINA: Freud's underrated. You were saying?

ELI: What was I saying?

ZARINA: The inner city. Marx.

ELI: Right. So my dad was into black culture. He loved jazz. We had a portrait of John Coltrane up in our dining room. His whole life was about bettering the plight of the black man, as he called it. And when I say he took it seriously? Where we lived there wasn't a single white family. All my friends growing up were black. They looked out for me, but I was still the white kid. I guess it's not surprising I've always felt like an outsider. Tupac and Public Enemy.

ZARINA: Instead of Dave Matthews and Jeff Buckley.

ELI: Exactly.

ZARINA: I'm a Jeff Buckley gal.

ELI: Hallelujah.

Pause.

ZARINA: So the Muslim thing fits in how exactly?

ELI: I'd been around Islam my whole childhood. The older Muslim guys, those were the guys I looked up to. Then I read Malcolm. Have you read *The Autobiography*?

ZARINA: I haven't...

ELI: You should.

ZARINA: I've a lot to read.

ELI: Of course. With your own writing. I want to hear all about that.

ZARINA: I don't talk about it.

ELI: Right...

Awkward pause.

ZARINA: Look, I barely know you. I'm doing this for my father.

ELI: I was surprised to find you on that site. I know we didn't talk much at the Hirsi Ali event, but it didn't seem in character —

ZARINA: It isn't.

ELI: Me neither.

ZARINA: But you were on it...

ELI: I have a friend who met someone on that site, and now he's very happily married. I thought I'd try it.

ZARINA: I don't think you and my dad would make such a great couple.

ELI: I should've figured it out. I'm embarrassed.

ZARINA: You should be.

ELI: He kept the messages short, though he did keep sending me these really elaborate emoticon smiley faces.

ZARINA: He means well.

ELI: So you're not having any fun at all?

ZARINA: I didn't say that.

> *(Beat)*
>
> So what was it about Malcolm?

ELI: The rage. That profound, righteous rage. I remember one night, I was seventeen. I was staying with my grandparents in upstate New York. I'd just read that section in *The Auto-biography* where Malcolm is discovering the history of white colonial power. That night at dinner, I was railing at my grandparents about the white man and what he'd done...

> At one point my grandmother says, very nicely: "But Eli, you're white." And I remember saying: "Yeah. Well, I don't have to be. Not like that."

ZARINA: Wonderful.

ELI: So I got *that* Malcolm. But it was the other Malcolm, the post-hajj Malcolm, who taught me that, at its core, Islam is really about being equal. Which is what he realized when he went to Mecca. Muslims of all colors, incomes, languages... Worshipping. Together.

> *Hearing this causes Zarina visible agitation.*

ZARINA: Where's the dark side?

ELI: Excuse me?

ZARINA: Maybe your grandma was onto something. White kid doesn't want to be white so badly, realizes the only way he can do it is to become Muslim?

ELI: Don't you think that's a little...

ZARINA: What?

ELI: Reductive. Condescending.

ZARINA: Or direct.

ELI: You're more like your dad than you realize.

ZARINA: I'll take that as a compliment.

ELI: Take it any way you want.

Beat.

ZARINA: We should get the check.

ELI: I'm sorry. I didn't mean to—

ZARINA: It's fine.

ELI: You push at me, I push back...and you want the check?

ZARINA: Look. You seem like a great guy. I'm just not—

ELI *(Interrupting)*: What did I say? Did I say something wrong?

Pause.

ZARINA: All that stuff about Islam. Equality and all that bullshit.
     You didn't have to grow up as a woman inside it.

ELI: You're right, I didn't.
     (Beat)
     Tell me about your writing.

ZARINA: I don't talk about my writing.

ELI: Why not?

Pause.

ZARINA: I'm writing a novel.

ELI: What's it about?

ZARINA: Gender politics.

ELI: And then what happens?

ZARINA: It's about the Prophet.

About the day that he married Zaynab bint Jahsh. Wife number seven. Who is the reason for the revelation of the veil. The curtain.

ELI: And a very beautiful woman, apparently...

ZARINA: Right, but who, before becoming the Prophet's wife, was actually his daughter-in-law—

ELI: But married to his *adopted* son.

ZARINA: Do you know the story about how, before the divorce, the Prophet saw Zaynab naked?

ELI: That story has been completely discredited.

ZARINA: The problem, Eli, is that it's in Tabari and alluded to in the Quran. Everyone is always trying to whitewash the sources—

ELI: The Prophet's not perfect. Nobody said he—

ZARINA: Right. Because of that time that he, like, frowned at some blind guy. So a chapter in the Quran gets named "He Frowned" and we're supposed to be so impressed at how revealing he is about his failings. But when it might be something truly human, like a man at war with his own desire, everyone's so eager to airbrush that out.

(Beat, increasingly passionate)

What's the big deal? Contradictions only make him more human, which only makes him more extraordinary.

(Catching herself)

Anyway. That's how my novel starts. With the Prophet seeing Zaynab naked, with him wrestling with his desire for his son's wife.

ELI: Intense.

ZARINA: Yeah.

ELI: I mean you.

(Beat)

Tell me more.

ZARINA: Most of my book takes place the day of their eventual
wedding...—You know what, I'm not sure it's your cup of tea.

ELI: Try me.

Beat.

ZARINA: I'm using that day to show the different influences on the
Prophet's life. And how the Quran is the result of all these
very human things that are happening to him. His problems
with his wives, his community, his own anxieties...In a lot
of ways, I think it might make more sense to see the Quran
more as coming from Muhammad than God.

ELI: I see.

ZARINA: Do you know the account of the wedding in Tabari?

ELI: I mean—I'm sure I read about it at some point, but...

ZARINA: Well, after the Prophet's son and Zaynab get divorced,
there is trouble in the community because the Prophet wants
to marry her. So to calm everybody down, Muhammad
throws a big party the day of the wedding. But the party
goes on too long. The Prophet doesn't want to kick people
out, the whole point had been to appease them, but this is
his *wedding* night.

ELI *(Wryly)*: Right.

ZARINA: So finally the Prophet gets up and starts walking to the
bedroom, where Zaynab is waiting. And one of the guests,
not realizing where the Prophet's going, follows him. Muhammad has had it. He gets to the bedroom, stops cold, and pulls
shut the curtain covering the entrance. And with that curtain
between them, the Prophet recites the famous verses:
Believers.

37

Do not enter the house of the Prophet at improper times.

Do not engage in familiar talk. This would annoy the Prophet and he would be ashamed to ask you to go.

If you ask the Prophet's wives for anything, speak to them from behind a curtain.

(Beat)

You know the Arabic word for curtain.

ELI: Hijab.

ZARINA: And because of Muhammad's very human impatience to be with his wife, generations and generations of Muslim women wear a curtain to his bedroom on their faces. I mean, really?

ELI: Well it's not the only reason.

ZARINA: The other references in the Quran, Eli, are even more dubious.

ELI: There are a lot of young women who wear the veil in my mosque and are proud of it.

ZARINA: They can be proud. As long as they understand they're turning themselves into metaphorical wives of the Prophet.

ELI: What's wrong with that? If they see it as a sign of devotion…?

ZARINA: You want to show devotion, Eli? Why don't *you* start wearing a veil?

ELI: I was saving that for our second date.

(Beat)

Your book sounds amazing. I mean it. I want to read it.

ZARINA: I'm not done. Not nearly.

I've had writer's block. Took me two and a half years to get through a draft and it's all wrong. Haven't been able to write a word for six months.

ELI: Why not?

ZARINA *(With a shrug)*: I don't know.

ELI: I find that hard to believe. You probably have a pretty good idea.

ZARINA: If I did, why would I tell you?

ELI: Because...I'm here. And I'm interested. And—I'm just guessing—but you're going to probably end up not seeing me again, so you've got nothing to lose...

Beat.

ZARINA: I feel like I'm not letting myself...

I have this sense of Muhammad, of *who* he was. We know all these things about the Prophet. Or think we do, details: he was an Arab, Aisha was his favorite wife, he had a gap between his teeth, whatever. And all the stories we hear, that have gotten told for hundreds of years, don't point to a real person. It's all like this monument to *what* we have made of him. But *who* he really was?

We don't know.

(Beat)

That's what I'm calling it. *The Who and the What.*

ELI: It's incredibly ambitious. Depending on how you go about it, could be trouble.

ZARINA: And with what passes for blasphemy these days? How little it takes for there to be rioting in the streets. People setting things on fire.

ELI: It is disheartening.

Beat.

ZARINA *(Off a sigh)*: My father thinks I have fifteen biographies of the Prophet 'cause I love him so much.

ELI: He did mention that you had fifteen biographies.

ZARINA *(Shifting, off a sudden thought)*: You know what?

(Reaching for a "specials" card on the table)

I just had an idea…

Do you have a pen?

Act One: Scene Five

Night. The kitchen. Afzal, alone.

Picking through pictures in a shoe box, as the lush, plaintive sounds of a Mehdi Hassan ghazal play in the background.

He takes up a picture of his deceased wife, clearly moved. Kisses it.

As he quietly hums and mutters along to the ghazal under his breath.

When—Mahwish enters, keys in hand. A handbag over her shoulder.

MAHWISH: Dad?

AFZAL: Behti.

MAHWISH: Dad, why do you have that box out?

AFZAL: I'm missing her, Mahwish.

MAHWISH: Last time you—

AFZAL *(Coming in)*: I'm sixty years old. I'm entitled to look at pictures of my wife if I want to.

MAHWISH: Okay. But last time you got so depressed…

AFZAL *(Picking out a photo)*: Look at this one.

Mahwish approaches.

AFZAL (CONT'D): You were not born yet, behti. Summer of 1980.

MAHWISH: I know, Dad. When you and Mom went to Memphis.

AFZAL: Your mother had to see Graceland. For the life of me I
don't know what she saw in that man, but she was obsessed...

Beat.

MAHWISH: Zarina upstairs?

AFZAL: Not back.

MAHWISH: She's not back?

AFZAL: Not yet.

MAHWISH: Dad. That's a good sign.

AFZAL: I'm trying not to think about it, behti. Your sister is very
unpredictable.
   (Off a sudden thought)
   On the way back from Memphis, there was a catfish
farm. Your mother did some fishing for the first time. She
caught something. When she pulled it up, it was a turtle.
She was so surprised—

MAHWISH: That she fell on you, and then you fell in the pond.
Right.

Pause.

AFZAL: You could at least pretend you haven't heard some of
these stories before, Mahwish. It would bring your father
some happiness.

MAHWISH: Sorry, Dad.

AFZAL: And I didn't exactly fall. I stepped into the pond.

*Mahwish's phone rings. With a call from Haroon. Some-
thing unpleasant. And that Mahwish hides from her father.*

MAHWISH *(On the phone)*: Hey…

> I didn't see them…
>
> Haroon, I just got home.
>
> I can't. I have my test for nursing school.
>
> But the test is in two weeks.
>
> I'm not saying that.
>
> Fine. I'll check.
>
> I said I'll check.
>
> Bye.

Beat.

AFZAL: How was the movie?

MAHWISH: Fine.

AFZAL: Something about *She*?

MAHWISH: *Her,* Dad. And no. Haroon wanted to see the new Stallone.

AFZAL: Sylvester Stallone?

MAHWISH: Yeah, Dad.

AFZAL: When I first came to this country, *Rocky* was playing in the movie theaters. That was a movie. Who knew what a *stooge* Stallone would become.

Silence. Mahwish looks at photos.

AFZAL (CONT'D): A man likes to get his way, behti. But that doesn't mean you have to do what he wants to make him feel like he's getting what he wants.

MAHWISH: I know, Dad.

AFZAL: You do?

MAHWISH: Yeah.

AFZAL: How?

MAHWISH: I've had a lot of practice.

Beat.

AFZAL: Very cheeky.

Sounds of Zarina's return.

Hiding their eagerness to see how her evening has gone, Afzal and Mahwish bury themselves in the photos.

Zarina appears, keys in hand.

ZARINA: What are you guys doing?

AFZAL: Just looking at photos.

MAHWISH *(Pointing to a photo)*: Who's that, Dad?

AFZAL: That was your mother's cousin Soraya.

ZARINA *(Knowing)*: You guys were waiting up for me.

AFZAL: No.

MAHWISH: I just got back from a movie.

ZARINA: Okay. Well, good night.

As Zarina turns to go…

MAHWISH: How was it?

ZARINA: Good.

AFZAL: Good?

ZARINA: Yeah. I—uh—actually had some ideas. I need to get upstairs.

Beat.

AFZAL: Okay.

Zarina moves off. Stops just as she is about to exit…

ZARINA: Hey, Dad. Thank you.

AFZAL: Okay, behti.

ZARINA: K. Night.

AFZAL: Night.

Afzal and Mahwish watch her go. Delighted.

Lights Out.

Then Lights Up —

Zarina's room. A desk. A computer. And pages.

Zarina pulls out the card on which she has written sentences.

ZARINA *(Reading)*: What if it wasn't God speaking to him? What if it was just his own voice?

And then begins writing.

ZARINA (CONT'D): How could he know if his thoughts were his own or his Lord's? Sometimes the voice he heard was soft — no, sometimes the voice he heard was *tender* and brought to mind his mother, the sweet long-missing comfort.

At times he could've sworn it was a woman speaking to him. He could have sworn the Lord was a woman.
(Pause)

Why did everyone need him to pretend he didn't have doubts? Why couldn't he show himself to them as he was?

As she continues…

Lights Up On—

Afzal. Laying out his prayer rug. For evening prayer. And as he begins praying,

Zarina, in her room, keeps writing:

ZARINA (CONT'D): If only he could forget the image of Zaynab's breasts. His desire for her was not to be avoided. For then they would all know what kind of man he truly was. Then they would know to turn not to him, a man, but to the Lord, their God.

Afzal bows and prostrates.

End of Act One.

Act Two: Scene One

One year later.

Morning.

Zarina and Eli. At home. Both wearing wedding bands on their ring fingers.

ELI: I said I was sorry.

ZARINA: Why were you drinking cranberry juice, anyway?

ELI: Why do you care what I was drinking?

ZARINA: You never drink cranberry juice—

ELI: I didn't intend to spill my drink—

ZARINA: What are you, on your period?

ELI: Zarina.

ZARINA: The sweater's ruined.

ELI: I said I was sorry.

ZARINA: If you weren't sitting next to that harpy. Waving your hands around like a friggin' windmill—

ELI: She's Haroon's sister. She's my family now, too.

ZARINA: She's a harpy.

ELI: And I wasn't waving my hands around like a—

ZARINA *(Coming in)*: And you should know by now, Haroon's father isn't going to donate to the mosque—

ELI: You've made *that* very clear.

ZARINA: He didn't even give us a check for our wedding. So there's no need to kiss his ass. One thing we don't do in this family? Is kiss Haroon's family's ass.

ELI: I wasn't kissing his ass.

(Pause, considering)

Is this about your...

ZARINA: You can't even bring yourself to say it.

Beat.

ELI: I wanted to make sure we had the space and time to have the conversation—

ZARINA *(Over)*: Eli! You finished reading the book two days ago! You didn't even tell me.

ELI: I've been sharing you with this book for an entire year. I don't get two days to think about it?

ZARINA: When people love something? They tell you. When they don't? They need time to *think* about it.

ELI: I couldn't put it down. I finished it at three a.m.

ZARINA: And if you'd loved it, you would've woken me up.

Pause.

ELI: Your portrayal of the Prophet is stunning. That searching quality, his constant self-questioning, his rich conflicted inner life. You really put me in the head of this man...

ZARINA: Which is what I was trying—

ELI: But he's nothing like the man I know. I didn't recognize him, Zarina. I didn't recognize the man I fell in love with when I became a Muslim. I mean the man in your book is overwhelmed. He's not always clear if he's hearing voices or going crazy or if it's God speaking to him. He's confused about his desires. We see him maneuvering for political advantage—

ZARINA: And he's charismatic and inspiring and generous, too.

(Beat)

I thought you understood what I was doing.

ELI: I do.

ZARINA: Apparently not.

Beat.

ELI: I'm concerned. It's very convincing. You're a very good writer, Zarina. And I'm worried that what you're putting out there is going to make people who don't know...—make them think that's who the Prophet really was.

ZARINA: Nobody knows *who* the Prophet really was. We hear these stories from our parents—

ELI: Yes, and the man in those stories matters to people. They think they know him. They love that man. The one who goes to visit the old woman who threw garbage on him every day on his way to the mosque—

ZARINA: Really?—

ELI: —knocks on her door on the one day that she doesn't dump trash on him, finds her sick in bed, and spends the day taking care of her. A woman who wished him nothing but ill.

ZARINA: And George Washington didn't actually chop down a cherry tree, Eli.

ELI: Does it matter? If the story makes people want to be more honest? Or more compassionate? Who cares if it's—Isn't that the deeper truth?

ZARINA: No. It's not.

ELI: Well, I don't know if I agree with you.

Pause.

ZARINA: You encouraged me.

ELI: I just didn't realize…how much you hated the man.

ZARINA: I don't hate him.

I hate what the faith does to women. For every story about his generosity or his goodness, there's another that's used as an excuse to hide us. Erase us. And the story of the veil takes the cake.

ELI: I get it, but the young men and women in my mosque…the people you're trying to reach? If they don't recognize the man you're writing about, they're not going to listen to you.

Long pause.

ZARINA: God. All that time. And if the person I dedicated it to doesn't even…

ELI: I have a lot at stake. The congregation…
(Beat, going to her)
Zarina.

ZARINA: No. You don't get to touch me.

ELI: Why not?

ZARINA: Why would you want to touch someone who hates the Prophet so much?

Beat.

ELI: So should I not have said anything? If you didn't want to hear—

ZARINA *(Getting emotional)*: That's right, Eli. You shouldn't have said anything.
(Beat, reaching for manuscript)

Can I have it back?

ELI: No.

ZARINA: Why?

ELI: I was planning on reading it again. That's why I didn't want to talk about it yet.

ZARINA: If you hate it so much—

ELI: I don't hate it. Can't you see I'm conflicted? I mean—Isn't that what good art is supposed to do?

Pause.

ZARINA: That's sweet.

ELI: I'm not trying to be sweet.

ZARINA: It's still sweet.

Beat.

ELI: I love you.

ZARINA: You still do?

ELI: It's not just the congregation. I'm worried people won't understand what you're doing. And I don't want anything to happen to you.

Act Two: Scene Two

The same day. Sometime in the early afternoon.

Afzal's kitchen.

Eli under the sink. Afzal watches him from the counter.

AFZAL: How's it look?

ELI *(From under sink)*: Not so bad. It was just clogged.

AFZAL: What a luxury.

ELI: What's that?

AFZAL: A son-in-law who can fix anything.

ELI: You got lucky. My eleven o'clock canceled.

AFZAL: Good man, good man.

    (Beat)

    So what's happening with that award?

ELI *(Emerging from under the sink)*: It's official.

AFZAL: Young Muslim Leader of the Year?

ELI: So they say.

AFZAL: Quite an honor. You deserve it.

ELI: Well, they're not exactly my favorite organization in the world.

AFZAL: What's wrong with the Muslim Association of North America?

ELI: They're a little conservative. They like telling people what it means to be Muslim more than I'm comfortable with. To you, your Islam. To me, mine.

AFZAL: They're giving *you* their award. How conservative can they—

ELI: C'mon, Afzal. I'm a white convert.

AFZAL: So what?

ELI: You're really gonna pretend you don't know what I'm talking about?

AFZAL: Those who come to the faith of their own will, that's a very special thing—

ELI: Doesn't seem so special when African Americans do it. Am I wrong?
(*Off Afzal's silence*)
But when a white guy does it? Suddenly it's like the Red Sea parts.

AFZAL: Look...
It's always an honor when one of your kind chooses our way of life. We'll take our rare victories in these dark times.

ELI: Yeah, well. It bothers me.

AFZAL: Why? You're the one reaping the benefit. Enjoy it—
(*Suddenly remembering*)
Oh...

Afzal pulls an envelope from his back pocket. Lays it on the counter.

ELI: What's that?

AFZAL: Cash.

ELI: For what?

AFZAL: For services rendered.

ELI *(Checking the envelope)*: Afzal. How much is this?

AFZAL: Five thousand.

ELI: Five thousand. For the sink?
(Handing it back to Afzal)
We've been through this before. I'm fine.

AFZAL: Yes, we have been through it. You're not fine. You need the money. Both of you.

ELI: We don't.

AFZAL: Eli. My daughter is not used to wanting for things. Just take it.

ELI: No disrespect, but if the money's for her, you should give it to her directly.

Afzal looks at Eli, askance.

AFZAL: Money is a man's matter. It is out of respect for you—as a man—that I am giving it to you and not her.

ELI: I appreciate that. And as a man, I'm telling you I don't want it.

AFZAL: What's the big deal?

ELI: No.

AFZAL: Come on.

ELI: Afzal!

AFZAL: Put it into the mosque if you don't want it for your family. Put it into the soup kitchen. I don't care.

ELI: You're already building us an addition.

AFZAL: And happy to be doing it. Couldn't be happier. What does the Prophet say? Build a house of God and you've built your own in heaven.

ELI: Appreciated by lots of us down here below, too.

AFZAL: You won't take the driver. You won't take the money.

55

ELI: Don't need a driver. I drive myself.

AFZAL: You know how many knuckleheads I've got on payroll listening to their iPods and playing video games all day long? Might as well put them to work.

ELI: Doesn't look good for the Imam to be driven around.

AFZAL: Just thought it might help…

ELI: Help with what?

Beat.

AFZAL: For what it's worth, a woman likes to know she's with a man, Eli.

ELI: Right.

AFZAL: I know my daughter. She needs to feel protected, by a strong man. With a strong hand. Cash doesn't hurt. It can make up for some of the other things…

ELI: Other things?

AFZAL: You think I don't see what's going on between the two of you?

(Beat)

    She has the power. She has the power she shouldn't have.

ELI: What are you talking about?

AFZAL: Fine. Fair enough. You're right. You're right. I should mind my own business.

ELI: Yes. You should.

AFZAL: So there is a problem.

ELI: You're really something.

AFZAL: What's going on? Just tell me. I can help you.

ELI: Nothing.

AFZAL: At the function last night. With the cranberry juice. What was all of that?

ELI: Miscommunication.

AFZAL: I would never let a woman speak to me like that in public.

ELI: She's been a little stressed.

AFZAL: About what?

ELI: She just finished her book, and—

AFZAL *(Coming in)*: Thank God she finally got that out of her system! Now she can concentrate on something that actually matters. Children.

ELI: I wouldn't hold your breath.

AFZAL: Why not?

ELI: She's not sure she wants kids.

AFZAL: What the hell—

What the hell does what she wants...

Just be a man. Put it in her. Get her pregnant. Women don't always know what they want.

ELI: She's on birth control.

AFZAL: Birth control? She's already thirty-three. It's not going to get any easier. She doesn't have that much time left...

She's headstrong. Just headstrong. We both know where it comes from, but the truth is, what's an advantage in a man isn't always in a woman. It can be an impediment to a woman's happiness.

She's my daughter. I know her. She needs room to breathe. But not too much room.

She has more power over you than she really wants. She can't help it.

And she won't be happy until you break her, son. She needs you to take it on, man.

ELI *(Indignant)*: Break her?

AFZAL: Don't act so offended.

ELI: I am offended.

AFZAL (*Interrupting*): Well that's part of the problem. You need some breaking, too. You're too passive.

ELI: Women don't need to be broken. They need to be heard.

AFZAL: Fine.

ELI: Seen. Respected.

AFZAL: Forget the generalizations. Okay?

I'll grant you I don't know anything about women. Not. A. Thing.

But I know about us. Where we come from.

Zarina's not an American girl. You understand that, right? I mean, she is, in some ways. But not in others.
(*Beat*)
Her mother's family was from Frontier. You know Frontier Province, right?

ELI: Sure.

AFZAL: They are not the most progressive people, Eli. More loyal you will never find. Willing to give you everything they have. A Pashtun friend? A friend for life. They are a wonderful people. Just a little backward.

Now Zarina's mother—bless her soul—she was not like that. And her mother's mother was not like that. But she grew up around cousins and uncles and aunties who were. There are women on that side of the family, I've never seen their faces.

Zarina's mother? Hated the veil. She never wore it. But the structure of that culture, the man at the center, that was in her bones. And you know what? It helped me. She needed

me to become stronger. To be more of a man. I had to find it
in myself. She made me. She made my success possible.
(Beat)

   Marriage is a mysterious thing, Eli. Mysterious and magical.

Eli is listening. Making his own connections.

AFZAL (CONT'D): I know what you're thinking: Zarina is different. She's not.

   She is her mother's daughter. Sure, she's brilliant. We
know that. I mean when they gave her that IQ test in fourth
grade, nobody could believe the score. She probably got that
from her mother's side, but don't get me wrong. There was
nobody that smart anywhere in the family.

   When her mother died…

   And after what happened with that Ryan…

ELI: Ryan.

AFZAL: She told you all about that…

ELI: Some guy she dated in grad school?

AFZAL *(Surprised)*: Dated? She didn't…

ELI: What?
   (Beat)
       Afzal?

AFZAL: What?

ELI: What is it?

AFZAL: If it's not…Then it's not my place to—

ELI: It's your place to give me advice on breaking your daughter,
   but not to tell me about what happened with Ryan?

Afzal considers.

AFZAL: I didn't know what it was, dating. We don't have it. With Mahwish it was never a problem. She always had that boy Haroon. Who I knew since he was a child. Now they're married.

(Beat)

In college, if Zarina did some dating, she never told me. I'm sure she told her mother things. But they never mentioned to me. When Zarina was getting her MFA, she met this...Ryan. She didn't tell me until her mother was very sick. And then her mother died.

(Beat)

I thought—at the time—it was something she needed. I didn't stop it. Not right away. That was my mistake. Either I should have stopped it or allowed it.

ELI: What happened?

AFZAL: He came to Atlanta, Christmas 2009. A solid fellow. Catholic. Irish. You know the type. But very smart. Could keep up with that mind of hers. Like you.

He came to my office. Very respectful. Asked for her hand in marriage.

ELI: They wanted to get *married?*

AFZAL: Over my dead body. That's what I told him. Zarina cried that night. Oh my God, she cried. But when it was over, it was over.

Pause.

ELI: When what was over?

AFZAL *(Perhaps with a hint of pride)*: She broke up with him.

Just like the Prophet's daughter did. Left the man she loved, because he wouldn't become a Muslim.

ELI: Right.

Pause. Eli is visibly troubled.

AFZAL: Eli...

Pause.

ELI: I—uh—I need to step outside. I need some air.

Afzal watches him go. Regretful.

His gaze comes to rest on Eli's bag.

Afzal has an idea. Stepping over, he takes out the envelope of cash from his pocket and slips it into the bag. But as he does, he notices something. He reaches inside and pulls out Zarina's manuscript. Looking at the cover.

He looks up in the direction in which Eli walked off. Then back down at the pages in his hands. Which he now peruses. Confused. Surprised. And not pleasantly.

He looks up again. Then slips the manuscript into a kitchen drawer.

Act Two: Scene Three

Zarina on her couch.

Mahwish stands beside her, looking worried.

ZARINA: What were you doing in Decatur? That's nowhere near —

MAHWISH *(Coming in)*: They have great coffee there.

ZARINA *(Skeptical)*: Wish.

MAHWISH: Okay. Manuel usually hangs out there after class. I mean he did last year.

ZARINA: So what happened?

MAHWISH: He asked me if I wanted to see his place. He lives around the corner from that coffee shop.

(Beat)

We went up the stairs. He went into the kitchen and got me an ice tea. When he gave it to me, our hands touched. It was amazing. And then he kissed me.

ZARINA: Manuel kissed you?

MAHWISH: God. It was like our lips melted into each other.

(Beat)

I had to go. I had nursing class. I went outside. There's this magnolia tree in his courtyard. That pink against the blue sky. Everything looked different.

Pause.

ZARINA: So you're not leaving anything out?

MAHWISH: Well, we made out.

ZARINA: So you didn't sleep with him?

MAHWISH: Of course not! Zarina! Is that what you think of me? That I would sleep with Manuel?

ZARINA: I wouldn't judge you if you did.

MAHWISH: I would judge myself.

Beat.

ZARINA: I mean, you did marry the only guy you ever kissed, Wish.

Pause.

MAHWISH: When we were kids, remember how you always used to say you wanted to marry Dad when you grew up...

ZARINA: Yeah...

MAHWISH: I thought I was going to marry the Prophet. I know it's deranged. But that's how kids are. Things don't have to make sense, right?

'Cause Mom told me—I was like seven—that the Prophet met Aisha when she was nine, and she ended up becoming his favorite wife. So I got it in my head that when I was nine, I was going to become the Prophet's favorite wife, too...

You know what happened when I turned nine?

I met Haroon. That's when Yasmin *chachi* moved from Pakistan to South Carolina. That's when he and I first met.

That was the sign.

He was wearing that white turtleneck and those Levi's. You remember that?

ZARINA: I don't.

MAHWISH: He was seriously cute.

ZARINA: Yes he was.

Beat.

MAHWISH: I mean he still is.
(*Off Zarina's silence*)
Because if it wasn't meant to be, then everything in between has just been wasted time...
(*Pause*)
Zarina, I can't stop wondering what Mom would think of me.

Mahwish's phone sounds with a text.

ZARINA: That him?

MAHWISH: Dad. He wants me to come over.

ZARINA: For what?

MAHWISH: I don't know.
Right now, it's not really a betrayal, right? It's just a lark.

ZARINA: I can tell you saw him just from your vocabulary.

MAHWISH: I mean it's not as bad as it would be...

ZARINA: If?

MAHWISH: I do it again.

ZARINA: I say, do what you want.

MAHWISH: What if I don't know what I want?

Beat.

ZARINA: When you think of Haroon...what do you think of?

MAHWISH: He's my husband.

ZARINA: But what is it about him?

MAHWISH: Oh. He's smart.

ZARINA: Yeah.

MAHWISH: And funny.

ZARINA: Mmm...

MAHWISH: No, he is. He's different around you. You intimidate him.

ZARINA: Okay.

(Beat)

What else?

MAHWISH: He never does any dishes...but he always buys me Pinkberry.

ZARINA: Okay.

MAHWISH: And he's got such a great job.

ZARINA: Okay...

So if you take *away* all those things...

MAHWISH: Yeah?

ZARINA: And if you think of him. Of *who* he is. Just him.

MAHWISH: Yeah.

ZARINA: Not *what* you can say *about* him.

MAHWISH: Uh-huh.

ZARINA: How do you *feel* then?

MAHWISH: Feel?

ZARINA: Yeah.

Pause. Mahwish shrugs.

MAHWISH: I...

ZARINA: Just try.

Mahwish closes her eyes.

Beat.

They open, with a sudden thought.

ZARINA (CONT'D): Yeah?

MAHWISH *(Realizing)*: Mad. I feel mad.

ZARINA: Maybe that's why you ended up at Manuel's place.

Just as we hear sounds offstage.

And Eli enters with his bag...

ELI: Hey.

ZARINA: Hey.

Eli comes over to kiss Zarina. She offers her cheek.

ELI: Hey, Mahwish.

MAHWISH *(Gathering her things)*: Hey, Eli.
(To Zarina)
   I'm heading off...

ZARINA: Home?

MAHWISH: Stop by Dad's first.

ELI: Well, the kitchen sink's working now...

MAHWISH: Didn't know it wasn't before.

ZARINA: What was wrong with the sink?

ELI: Just a clog. Nothing serious.

MAHWISH *(To Zarina)*: I bet Dad clogged it just so he would come by and fix it.

ELI: Huh.

ZARINA: He was always disappointed he never had sons.

MAHWISH: Well, he's got one now! Bye.

Mahwish exits.

ZARINA: How's Dad?

ELI: He tried to give me money again.

ZARINA: Get used to it, honey. He makes money. He gives it away. That's the meaning of his life.

ELI: Certain elegance to it.

ZARINA: Absolutely.

(Beat)

So?

ELI: What?

ZARINA: How much?

ELI: Zarina. I didn't take it.

ZARINA: Why not?

ELI: It makes me uncomfortable.

ZARINA: Why?

ELI: I feel like it diminishes me.

Eli considers her for a long moment.

ZARINA: Okay. I'm sorry I was such a pain this morning.

ELI: It's fine.

ZARINA: No, it's not. You were just being honest. I was making it difficult for you to do what I asked you to do.

(Beat)

If you can't take me at my worst, you don't deserve me at my best. Right?

ELI: Why are you quoting Marilyn Monroe?

Beat.

ZARINA: What's wrong?

Pause.

ELI: Mahwish was sure in a hurry. Everything okay?

ZARINA: I probably shouldn't say anything.

ELI: About what?

Zarina hesitates.

ELI (CONT'D): Fine, don't tell me.

ZARINA: Okay...

There was this GRE instructor she had a crush on. I told her to get it out of her system before she got married.

ZARINA (CONT'D): She went to the coffee shop where he hangs out and ended up back at his place. They kissed.

ELI: So she liked this guy more than Haroon, but she married Haroon anyway.

ZARINA: I mean, it was a crush—

ELI: She gonna have an affair with this GRE instructor?

ZARINA: It wouldn't be the worst thing. She's not happy.

ELI: That seems incredibly destructive.

ZARINA: It's better than sitting around for years wondering what it would have been like...

Words that land hard on Eli.

ELI: Right.
(Beat)
Is there a reason you never told me about what happened with Ryan?
(Off Zarina's silence)
Your father mentioned it. He assumed I knew what he was talking about.

ZARINA: What did he say?

ELI: You wanted to get *married*.

> *(Off Zarina's silence)*
> Zarina.

ZARINA: Yes.

ELI: Why didn't you tell me?
> *(Off Zarina's silence)*
> Are you still in love with him?

ZARINA: It's over.

ELI: So why didn't you tell me?
> *(Silence)*
> Do you still have feelings for him?

ZARINA: Eli…

ELI: You do.

ZARINA: Stop it.

ELI: God. I'm an idiot.

ZARINA: Why are you saying that?

ELI: I wake up every morning and I feel so lucky to be with you.

ZARINA: I feel the same.

ELI: It's not the same. If it wasn't for your dad, you wouldn't be with me. You'd be married to somebody else!

ZARINA: But I'm not. I'm with you.

Pause. Eli roils inwardly.

ELI: At the Nikah ceremony—I had this moment—we were signing the certificate—I saw you…Some part of you wasn't mine. But I thought it would be. Someday. With time. I just didn't realize it was because you were in love with some other guy—

ZARINA: I'm not—

ELI: Why don't I believe you?

ZARINA: I don't know who Ryan is anymore! He's just an idea in my head! It's not about me being in love.

Dad made me end it. And I did. Just like that. I wouldn't talk to Ryan. I never saw him again. I shut the whole thing off. Shut myself off.

ELI: Are you with me to make your dad happy?

ZARINA: Of course not.

ELI: Are you in love with me?

Pause.

ZARINA: When we met, all I had was that book. After Mom died, after Ryan, that book was it. You know what changed? You came into my life. You are what changed it. I thought: Here's somebody I can actually be with.

ELI: Be with?

ZARINA: Eli, stop it.

ELI: I can't believe this is happening...

ZARINA: You were right. You just needed to give me time. That's all I need. Time.

ELI: I can't...I need to...

Eli picks up the bag and starts to exit.

ZARINA: Where are you going?

ELI *(Noticing something in his bag)*: Unbelievable.
    (Pulling the envelope of cash)
        I wouldn't take it, so he just stuffs it into my bag.
    (Searching through the bag)
        Wait a second.

ZARINA: What?

ELI: Your manuscript.
    (Still searching through the bag)
       I had it with me when I left the *masjid*. But it's not…
ZARINA: What?
ELI: Your dad…

Zarina and Eli share a worried look.

Act Two: Scene Four

Afzal's kitchen.

Mahwish stands across from her father, Zarina's manuscript open before her.

She is reading aloud.

MAHWISH: Do I still treat him like a boy? *he wonders as he pushes open the door to the courtyard.* Is that the cause of his strife with Zaynab? I know her feelings for me; I know my own for her. *He stops.* It is wrong for you to want her like this. There is something wrong with you.

AFZAL *(Underneath)*: Tauba, Allah, Tauba…

MAHWISH *(Continuing without interruption)*: *Approaching the door, he hears something inside.* "Zayd?" *he calls out to his son. There is no answer. He knocks. The door yawns open. There is Zaynab. Scurrying through the room, undressed.*

Mahwish stops. Looks up at her father, alarmed. Then goes on, suspiciously.

MAHWISH *(CONT'D)*: "Come in, Father," *she says. He has no words to reply. His stomach hurts with the pain of not*

having her. Through the window, he sees her, her breasts, full and startling...
(Stopping)

Oh my God.

MAHWISH (CONT'D): Dad. What is she thinking?

AFZAL: She's *not* thinking. I've been too soft on that girl. Letting her pine away in that ivory tower.

Mahwish puts down the manuscript.

As if it were something unholy.

AFZAL (CONT'D): What did you know about this?

MAHWISH: Nothing.

AFZAL: You knew nothing?

MAHWISH: Dad. Of course not.

AFZAL: You mean to tell me you never asked her...?

MAHWISH: I did. She never wanted to say much.

AFZAL: Now we know why.

Beat.

MAHWISH: The most I ever got from her was that it was gender politics.

AFZAL: Gender politics?

MAHWISH: Relationships between men and women.

AFZAL: What does that have to do with politics?

MAHWISH: It's just a term, Dad.

AFZAL: It was something to do with politics?

MAHWISH: No, it's not—

AFZAL: You should have told me. I'm your father.

MAHWISH: I'm sorry.

AFZAL: You never told me your sister was sex-crazed.

MAHWISH: I mean...she's not.

AFZAL: Then why is she writing these things? Hmm?

MAHWISH: I don't know. We have to talk to her.

AFZAL *(Over)*: It's unacceptable! Completely unacceptable! I won't stand for it!

MAHWISH: Calm down, I'm sure she'll—

AFZAL: In Pakistan? She would be killed for this. Killed. If anybody gets their hands on this, God forbid...
(Getting emotional)
    If anything happened to her, to either of you...

MAHWISH: Dad. Stop it. It'll be fine.

AFZAL: How do I know that?

MAHWISH: Nothing's gonna happen.

AFZAL: How do you know that?! Can you promise me that? Can you? Hmm?

All at once, Afzal looks as though he's on the verge of a panic attack.

Mahwish goes to him.

Just then, we hear sounds offstage.

Zarina and Eli appear.

MAHWISH: Zarina, you have to talk to him—

ELI: I think I may have left something—

AFZAL: You didn't leave anything. I took it.

ELI: You went into my bag...?

MAHWISH: Have you read this?

ELI: Yes I have.

AFZAL: You know about this and you carry it around in your bag? What kind of man are you? What kind of Muslim? You know about it and you do nothing to stop her?

ZARINA: Stop me?

AFZAL: What is wrong with you, man?

ZARINA: There's nothing wrong with him.

AFZAL: For God's sake, Zarina!

(Taking up the manuscript)

This? About the Prophet?! Have you lost your mind?

It's clear Afzal's anger is having an effect on his daughter.

ZARINA: Have you even read it, Dad?

Afzal stares at her for a long beat, then looks down at the manuscript and turns a few pages. He begins to read aloud now, his quiet voice trembling with anger.

MAHWISH: Dad, please don't.

AFZAL: *She lowers her head to offer her bare neck.*

MAHWISH: Zarina, get him to stop!

AFZAL: *She leans against the wall as he leans against her. He grows against her body—*

MAHWISH *(Over)*: Stop!

AFZAL: *—kissing her skin. She closes her eyes and moans, pushing into him, her neck against his mouth. His hands cup her breasts.*

MAHWISH *(Over)*: Dad, stop reading!

AFZAL *(Throwing the manuscript at Zarina)*: This is the Prophet!—peace be upon him—What did I do to deserve this!?

ZARINA: Dad, you can't just read a few sentences and think you know what it's about.

MAHWISH *(Coming in)*: What's it about, Zarina?

AFZAL: I don't care what it's about!

MAHWISH *(Emphatic)*: No! What's it about?!

AFZAL *(To Zarina)*: And for your information, I read more than a few sentences. God being a woman? God having breasts?

ZARINA: That's not what's in—

AFZAL: It is. I read it.

ELI: It's a metaphor, sir.

AFZAL: I don't care what it is! God does not have breasts!

ELI: I'm just trying to help.

AFZAL: Nobody asked you.

ZARINA: It's about the Prophet, Dad. And the Quran. And how what we think we know about those things is not real. Not human.

AFZAL: What nonsense are you talking…

MAHWISH: Dad. Let her speak.

ZARINA: I'm telling the story of when he married Zaynab bint Jahsh. She is the reason for the revelation of the veil.

MAHWISH: The veil?!

ZARINA: We don't understand so many things about our own history and traditions.

AFZAL: Where your mother came from, I don't even want to tell you what they would do to you.

ZARINA: This is not Frontier Province, Dad.

AFZAL: If anyone sees this, you will never be able to go to Pakistan. We will never be able to go to Pakistan. Never again.

ZARINA: That's what you care about?

AFZAL *(Yelling)*: That's not what I care about! *You* are what I care about! You think they can't hurt you here? Hmm?

ZARINA: Then so be it.

MAHWISH: What are you talking about?

ZARINA: We can't keep not saying things because we're afraid of what somebody's going to do.

Beat.

AFZAL: Behti, are you so unhappy that you don't care what happens to you?

ZARINA: You know what you said to me the night I told you I wanted to marry Ryan? You told me a story about the Prophet's daughter—

AFZAL: I know what I said, for God's sake!

ZARINA: —about how she gave up the man she loved because he wouldn't become a Muslim. Do you remember?

AFZAL: Just let it go!

ZARINA: You said the Prophet's daughter had done it and so should I.

AFZAL: Would you forget it!

ZARINA: The story you told me wasn't even right, Dad!

AFZAL: I don't know what you think—

ZARINA: You didn't even have the story right!

AFZAL: So what's the story? This pornography about the Prophet?!

ZARINA: Dad—

ELI: It's not pornography, sir.

AFZAL: Shut your bloody mouth!

ELI: I'll shut my mouth when you calm down, Afzal—

AFZAL *(To Eli)*: Call yourself an Imam. What kind of Imam doesn't care about his wife writing such things about the Prophet?!

ELI: I've got a congregation I have to worry about.

AFZAL *(To Eli)*: Bloody fake is what you are!

ZARINA: What you did with that story is what we do. Distort these tales. It's what we've done with the veil for a thousand years.

MAHWISH *(Dumbfounded)*: What do you care about the veil?!

AFZAL: I never made you girls wear anything like that! It has nothing to do with your life!

ZARINA: Nothing to do with my life? You covered me up, Dad. You erased me.

AFZAL *(Shocked)*: I did what?

ZARINA: And I let you.

Beat.

AFZAL: You write such filth about the Prophet, peace be upon him, and then you put the blame on me?

ZARINA: That's not what I'm —

AFZAL: You make me regret the day you were born.

ZARINA: Abu...Please...

MAHWISH: How can you do this to him?
    (Beat)
    Reading this actually makes me want to start wearing a veil. Just to purify myself of it.

ELI: Mahwish...

ZARINA: Purify yourself?

MAHWISH: And all these years, I've been taking your advice? Like you know something? —

ZARINA: Stop it.

MAHWISH *(Continuing)*: You know what? There's actually something wrong with you.

ELI: That's not helping.

MAHWISH: I don't have to listen to you!

(Snapping back to Zarina)

And you can pretty it up with a lot of expensive words and fancy books, but it's just filth.

ZARINA: Filth?

MAHWISH: That's all it is. Thank God Mom's not here to see it.

ZARINA: And what would she think of you having ten years of anal sex so your boyfriend wouldn't break up with you?

AFZAL: What?

MAHWISH: I don't know what she's talking about.

ZARINA: I've stood behind you since you were like, what, sixteen? For your sick I'm-so-dependent-on-a-man-that-I'll-let-him-violate-me-so-I-never-lose-him.

AFZAL (To Mahwish): What is she talking about—

ZARINA: This is my thanks?

MAHWISH: She's lying.

ZARINA (To Afzal): You never really liked Haroon for a reason, Dad.

MAHWISH: She's the one writing blasphemy!

ZARINA: He's a scumbag.

MAHWISH: She couldn't be with the man she loved so she sits around masturbating to the Prophet in a public library!

AFZAL: That boy made you do what with him?

Speechless, Mahwish breaks down. All the verification Afzal needs. He turns to Zarina:

AFZAL (CONT'D): Do you see what this is doing? Don't you see it?

(Beat)

When that cancer had finally eaten your mother alive, behti, when she was dying...I promised her. She was the center. I promised I would be the center to hold the family together.

(Pointing at the manuscript)

Don't you see what this is?

It's like that goddamn cancer!

ZARINA: Dad...how can you say that?

AFZAL: I have made so many sacrifices for this family. I have sacrificed so much for the two of you. For you to be happy.

(Beat)

You have to destroy this book.

Reaching the manuscript out to her.

ZARINA: You haven't heard anything I've said.

AFZAL: You'll write another book, behti. With more wisdom. I know you will.

ZARINA: It's four years of my life.

AFZAL: Something that will bring light into the world. Not this cancer. This darkness.

ZARINA: Don't ask me to do that.

AFZAL: I'll never ask anything of you again. You have to destroy it.

ELI: Absolutely not.

AFZAL: You again?

ELI: You made her act against her heart once before, but you won't do it again.

AFZAL: I told you to shut your bloody mouth!

ELI: Calm down, sir!

AFZAL: I'm not going to calm down!

ELI *(Suddenly shouting)*: Yes you are!

AFZAL: You nonentity!

ELI: What she's done is important! She's reminding us that the Prophet was just a man—

AFZAL *(Over)*: Us? You're no Muslim.

ELI *(Continuing)*: We say we don't worship him, but we do!

AFZAL *(Over)*: Blah! Blah! Blah! Blah! Blah!

ELI *(Continuing)*: And we're worshipping a fiction! We have no interest in knowing who he really was...

AFZAL: I know who he was!

ELI: No, you don't! None of us do! And all your daughter is doing—

AFZAL: Blasphemy.

ELI: No, testimony. To a complicated and remarkable man with conflicting emotions.

Afzal turns to Zarina. And finds her looking at Eli.

AFZAL: Don't tell me.

ELI *(Continuing)*: That's it. That's all it is. And her courage is one of the many reasons I'm so in love with your daughter.

AFZAL *(Coldly)*: Zarina.

Zarina, are you listening to me?

Zarina continues to hold Eli's gaze.

ZARINA *(Still looking at Eli)*: Eli. Let's go.

Eli goes to her. She takes his hand.

AFZAL: Zarina!!

He breaks down, at once imperious and vulnerable.

AFZAL (CONT'D): Behti, don't.
> *(Struggling)*
>> If you love me, behti...

ZARINA *(Emotional)*: Dad.

AFZAL: If you love me...

ZARINA: I do, Dad.

AFZAL: If you do —

ZARINA: I love you so much...

Zarina and Eli exit. As they go:

AFZAL: Zarina!

They are gone.

Long beat.

Afzal goes to a picture on the wall of his elder daughter. Turns and throws it into the sink, violently.

He looks up at Mahwish.

AFZAL (CONT'D): That girl. I don't ever want to hear her name in this house again.
> *(Off Mahwish's silence)*
>> Do you hear me?!
> *(Still no reply)*
>> I said do you hear me?!?

MAHWISH: Yes.

AFZAL: She is dead to me. Dead.

Afzal moves to go. But before exiting:

AFZAL (CONT'D) *(Quieter)*: Whatever you did with him, I don't want to talk about it... You don't have to go back to that bastard. You can have your room, behti. However long you need. Whatever you want.

Afzal goes.

Mahwish takes Zarina's picture from the sink and leaves.

End of Act Two.

Epilogue

A summer day. Two years later.

Afzal sitting on a bench at Java on the Park. Prayer beads in hand.

Beat.

Mahwish appears. With two cups of coffee. Handing one to her father.

MAHWISH: Here you go, Dad.

AFZAL: Thank you, behti. You take such good care of your old father.

MAHWISH: You're not old, Dad.

Afzal takes the cup. Sips. Makes a face.

AFZAL: No hazelnut?

MAHWISH: They were out. I got you vanilla instead.

Afzal grunts.

He sips. Quietly. As we hear a distinctive chirping.

AFZAL *(Pointing)*: That is a Kentucky warbler.

MAHWISH: What?

AFZAL: Over there, on that tree.

MAHWISH: How do you know?

AFZAL *(Showing his iPhone)*: There's an app for that.

MAHWISH: Yeah?

AFZAL: Tweeter.

MAHWISH: Dad, Twitter's not about bird-watching.

AFZAL: Not Twitter, behti. *Tweeter. Tweeter.* It's different.
(*Pulling out his phone*)
You want to see it?

MAHWISH: It's okay, Dad. I'll leave the *ornithology* to you…

Mahwish checks her phone.

AFZAL: Manuel?

MAHWISH: No.

AFZAL: So who is it?

MAHWISH: Nobody. It's just a bad habit.

AFZAL: How is that Manuel?

MAHWISH: He's fine.

Pause. Afzal sips his coffee and feels the breeze.

AFZAL: Your mother, bless her soul, when she was alive she always tried to get me to slow down. She wanted me to sell the business years ago. I should have listened to her sooner. The art of life, that was your mother's gift.

MAHWISH: I miss her too.
(*Beat*)
There are so many things I regret not saying to her.

AFZAL: Me too.

Again, the distinctive chirping.

AFZAL (CONT'D): In the afternoons, he hops around. Then, God only knows what gets into him, he jumps up on that branch, always on that one, starts his song. He's a good friend now.

MAHWISH: How do you know he's a he?

AFZAL: I don't. I should check that.

(Beat)

I thought it's the males who sing. To get the females.

MAHWISH: I don't know, Dad. Girls like to sing, too.

Mahwish's phone sounds with a text. She gets up. Looks around.

MAHWISH (CONT'D): Dad. I'm gonna use the restroom.

AFZAL: Okay, behti.

Mahwish moves off. Stopping to wait just long enough to see Zarina appear.

They exchange a nod. Then Mahwish moves off.

Zarina stands upstage, looking at her father.

She watches her father watch the bird for a beat. Moved.

Until she finally approaches.

ZARINA: Dad...

AFZAL *(Turning)*: That was quick, behti—

Seeing Zarina, Afzal is filled with sudden emotion.

He turns away.

ZARINA *(Approaching)*: Dad.

AFZAL: This is your sister, right? *That's* why she wanted to come with me today. She never comes with me...

Pause.

ZARINA: I needed to talk to you, Dad.

AFZAL: You think you can just come like that after two years? No. I can't talk to you now, Zarina. Go, please.

Another pause.

ZARINA: I'm moving, Dad.

Silence.

ZARINA (CONT'D): Eli and I are moving. To Oregon.

Another pause.

AFZAL: Why?

ZARINA: Dad. After what happened with the congregation, there's no reason for him to still be here.

AFZAL: What did you expect, Zarina? After what you wrote...

ZARINA: I know.

AFZAL: I lost so many of my drivers. Even after I told them I didn't agree with you. I told them. They wanted nothing to do with me. The things they said about you. I couldn't. I couldn't listen to it. I...I had to sell the business.
    (Beat)
    You know some of them came and broke the windows of the house.

ZARINA: I know, Dad.
    (Beat)
    I'm sorry.

AFZAL: Are you?

ZARINA: Yes. That you had to suffer because of something I did. Something I wrote.

AFZAL: It's not the windows, behti. I don't care about that. Or the business. It's you. You are what I care about.

ZARINA: I'm fine.

AFZAL *(Getting emotional again)*: Just for you to be happy. That's all I ever wanted. I come here, I sit and do *tasbih* every day. I pray for you to be safe, happy.

ZARINA: I am, Dad.

AFZAL: What?

ZARINA: Happy. Your prayers are working.

Beat.

AFZAL: The people say awful things about you, behti. That makes you happy?

ZARINA: Not only. They don't only say awful things.

Pause.

AFZAL: I read it. I read the bloody thing three times. I still don't understand. Why you had to—

ZARINA: Okay, Dad. I mean that's okay, right? Maybe you don't have to understand.

AFZAL: Does anybody understand it?

ZARINA: Yes. I've gotten so many letters. Emails.

AFZAL: From Christians.

ZARINA: No. From Muslims. Istanbul. Lahore. London. Omaha.

AFZAL: Saying what?

ZARINA: That it helped them.

AFZAL: Muslims?

ZARINA: Yes.

AFZAL: How?

ZARINA: That it…gave them permission…to ask questions.

AFZAL: I don't have any questions.

    (Beat)

        I have been so angry with you. So angry.

ZARINA: I know.

AFZAL: And helpless.

ZARINA: Helpless?

Afzal doesn't reply.

Beat.

As the Kentucky warbler comes on strong. Loud and proud.
Afzal points.

AFZAL: She's my friend.

ZARINA: Is she?

AFZAL: We go way back.

ZARINA: Is that right?

AFZAL: She misses me when I don't come.

    (Beat)

        A lot.

ZARINA: She misses you.

AFZAL: And I miss her.

Pause. Zarina gets emotional.

ZARINA: Dad…

Hearing her, Afzal may soften inwardly, but he doesn't show it.

Mahwish and Eli appear. Seeing the two of them talking.

MAHWISH: Everything okay over here...?

ZARINA: Yeah.

MAHWISH *(To Zarina)*: Did you tell him, Z?

AFZAL: She told me.

MAHWISH: Isn't it great? Nana-*abba!*

ZARINA: I hadn't gotten to that yet, Wish.

AFZAL: What?

MAHWISH: You're going to be a grandfather!

AFZAL: Who's going to be a grandfather?

MAHWISH: You, Dad?

AFZAL: Zarina?

ZARINA: It's true.

Afzal looks at Eli.

ELI: I took your advice, sir.

AFZAL *(To Zarina)*: How many months?

ZARINA: Four...

Afzal reaches over, kissing Mahwish. With a blessing.

AFZAL: *Bismillah...Bismillah...Bismillah...*

Then turning to Zarina. But unable to embrace her, over-whelmed with emotion.

Afzal finally breaks down. Hiding his face. Sitting.

MAHWISH: Dad...

AFZAL *(Through the tears)*: No, no...

Mahwish and Zarina look at each other.

MAHWISH: Dad?

AFZAL: No, please, no.
    (Off Mahwish's touch)
    Mahwish. Go, go, please.
    (Beat, still hiding his face)
    I don't want you here.

Zarina, Mahwish, Eli exit.

Afzal tries to collect himself. Still fighting the emotions.

He looks up at the heavens, his hands before him, Muslim-style, for a prayer.

AFZAL (CONT'D): *Allah hu Akbar*...
    Bismillah ar-Rahman ar-Rahim...
    Ya Allah...
    Please, please, please.
    I love her. I love her too much.
    Please understand. Please forgive me.

As Zarina creeps back in upstage. Hearing the rest.

AFZAL (CONT'D): Dear sweet *Allahmia*, please bless that child.
Give it a long, healthy, happy life. And please give that
child a strong love for you. Whatever anger you have with
Zarina, *ya Allah,* please don't make that child suffer for
what she did. If you can't forgive her, just don't take it out
on him.

(Beat)
 Inshallah, please let it be a boy.

Beat.

ZARINA *(With sass, defiance)*: Dad.

Afzal turns to see her.

ZARINA (CONT'D): It's a girl.

Lights Out.

THE PARTICULAR AND
THE UNIVERSAL

An Interview with Ayad Akhtar

In June 2013, theater professionals from all over the world gathered in Dallas for Theatre Communications Group's (TCG) annual conference, "Learn Do Teach." The following is an excerpted and condensed version of a conversation between playwright Ayad Akhtar and Gabriel Greene, La Jolla Playhouse's director of new play development. The interview was held during the conference.

Gabriel Greene: In January of 2012, I got a call late one night from my mother. She had attended a performance of [Ayad Akhtar's first play] *Disgraced,* and she said, "If you haven't heard of this writer, you have to remedy that immediately." I feel like that was the story of 2012 for you: you came seemingly out of nowhere. Your first novel, *American Dervish,* was published in January. That same month, *Disgraced* premiered in Chicago. A month later, your second play, *The Invisible Hand,* premiered in Saint Louis. *Disgraced* moved to New York and then won the Pulitzer Prize. It's like you had sprung, fully formed, from the head of Zeus. How do you process the craziness of this last year?

Ayad Akhtar: I don't know. I think I'm still processing it. I, of course, feel incredibly grateful for all of the attention that the work has gotten. At the age of fifteen I knew I wanted to be a writer. My parents are both doctors, and up until that point I'd been trained like a little automaton to repeat that "I'm going to be a neurosurgeon when I grow up." And this one high school teacher completely changed my life, and I knew I wanted to be a writer.

GG: In what way did that teacher reach out to you?

AA: It was a world literature class. She had changed so many kids' lives. When she came into class, she had this regal bearing that was *not* affectation. It was this resonance of someone who is firmly committed to authenticity, to living an authentic life. She got me thinking about the deeper questions of life, and it just struck me: the most extraordinary thing I could do was to give myself to that process of asking those questions and putting it into narrative form.

The other thing that she did was she introduced me to a lot of European modernism. And so I was reading, you know, Thomas Mann and Rilke and Kafka and the existentialists. I carried with me—for at least a good ten to fifteen years—this idea that writing in a universal way was writing like a continental European modernist. "Write what you know" is very good advice, but I didn't take it for a long time because I thought, "Well, what I know is not universal, and nobody's going to really care." It didn't seem worthy of this very high calling of the questions of the meaning of life and what have you. It took me a long time to work that out.

GG: *The Who & The What* was originally programmed as part of the Playhouse's DNA New Work Series. The conversation we had afterwards was fantastically moving and exciting—a wonderful dialogue with the audience—and you shared a story about that transformation from thinking that what you were writing wasn't worthy of sharing.

AA: I'm not sure exactly what the moment of realization was, but it was sometime in my early thirties that I started to sense that I was avoiding something about where I came from, about who I was. It was something I was avoiding in my work, but also something I was avoiding on the level of identity. I had enough presence of mind to realize that the best way to respond to this growing awareness was to just be still about it and to see what happened. And at some point, metaphorically speaking, I started to look over my shoulder at what I was running from. And at that moment there was this burst of creativity. I mean, it was an explosion. So the matter of working through personal psychological or identity issues actually happened through the work, or with the work. *American Dervish* came from that moment, *Disgraced* did, *The Who & The What* did, a novel I'm working on now, a film I'm writing now...all of that stuff came from that encounter.

GG: In rereading *Disgraced* and thinking about *The Who & The What,* I'm reminded of W. E. B. DuBois talking about double consciousness, the idea that people see themselves through the lens of the dominant culture. In an interview in *American Theatre* magazine, you talk about the ways in which Muslims are still very beholden to the way they're viewed in the West.

AA: I'm not an apologist. I'm not involved in PR about correcting some impression that people have of Islam. My position is that, as an artist, I have to have the freedom to wrestle with my demons and my raptures and those of my community, and to celebrate and criticize in equal measure. And the best way to tell a good story about the world that I come from is not to worry about the politics of representation, except insofar as it's relevant to the characters that I'm representing. That said, I think it's a very long story. For a few centuries now, the West has had a dominant discourse that defines the Muslim "other" in a way that allows the West to justify its political practices and its sense of moral superiority. And so, in a post-9/11 landscape, where the Muslim "other" is even more pejoratively defined, what is the role of a Muslim American artist of some visibility in that discursive environment? And my relationship to that question is by no means obvious. Even to me, to be honest.

Post–World War II, a dominant discourse among the Jewish American community was, "What's good for the Jews, what's bad for the Jews?" Meaning, "Let's not do things that are bad for the Jews." There's a similar thing going on now in the Muslim community, which is totally understandable. Unfortunately, I lose any credibility as an artist, not only with my audience but with myself, if I cater to a political ideology one way or the other. My calling is to try to tell the best, most truthful story in the most compelling way.

GG: Can you talk about the inspiration for *The Who & The What*?

AA: One day, I was taking a cab home and I saw—you know the little TVs they have in New York cabs?—I saw this ad for *Kiss*

Me, Kate and I thought to myself, "What is this obsession with *Taming of the Shrew*?" It makes no sense! The gender politics of that play have no resonance for today's audience. *I* understand them because that's where I come from, that's my culture. I mean, my mom is basically Kate! A nicer version, but, you know...So I thought to myself, "I should write a knockoff of *Taming of the Shrew*." Where there's two sisters, the older sister has sworn off love, the younger sister's got a boyfriend, she wants to marry him, their father says, "You're not marrying your boyfriend till your older sister gets married." Coming into this whole thing, I wanted to write a relationship play about Muslim American matrimonial mores. That's where the inspiration for the play came from. And then of course there's this other thing, which is a meditation on the Prophet, and how the Prophet's example affects how Muslims approach the questions of love and commitment and matrimony and relationships.

GG: As a writer whose job it is to interrogate things like ideologies—which by definition don't like to be interrogated—how do you hope to start a conversation?

AA: One of the great things about doing theater is that I can write a play, and then a group of students in Pakistan or Indonesia can sit around a table and read it, and then decide they want to do it. If they can't get a theater to do it, they can do it in a basement, and they can invite people over. I hope that folks find *The Who & The What* meaningful, entertaining, and interesting enough to engage with it. It's a different way of fostering dialogue. Writing a play is a completely different kind of engagement with the world because you're engaging other people to engage with the world.

The Enlightenment was spread in the seventeenth and eighteenth centuries through a process that was similar—basically what we now call book clubs. Folks would get together and read the latest by Voltaire, or by Rousseau, and would discuss it and then would pass the book to another person. And it's that sort of movement of consciousness through living dialogue and embodied exchange that I think is so central to the theater.

GG: Like *The Who & The What,* your play *Disgraced* also explores the concept of Muslim American identity in contemporary times, though it is less a comedy than *The Who & The What.* How have audiences responded to that play?

AA: There have been a lot of different responses. The one through line I've noticed is that people are incredibly moved by the play. This is going to sound very pretentious, but...I remember reading Aristotle on tragedy years and years ago, and his definition of catharsis has to do with expression of emotion through pity and terror. "Terror" being key. And terror, as he defines it in his paradigmatic anecdote, is when the Furies arrived onstage, *women were miscarrying in the aisles.* [*Laughter from the audience*] Right? Who wants to go to a theater like that, right? [*More laughter*] Well, I do!

But shocking for shock's sake is not particularly interesting to me, personally. When Aristotle is talking about women miscarrying in the aisles, he's talking about a religious sense of awe. In the Islamic tradition, the word for "God-fearing" is the same as for "awe of God." And if you can begin to provoke that numinous dimension for an audience, then I think you're actually trying to open them up to a deeper level of existence.

I am trying to write to the universal. That is what I'm trying to do, period. Stories that say "Muslim Americans and Muslims are people too" can't necessarily reach everybody in the audience where they live and breathe. It can illuminate things for them, but it can't necessarily force them to ask the deepest questions of their own lives. What I hope I'm discovering is that by writing from the particular that I know—that I find fascinating and that I have a lot of love for and a whole lot of problems with—I can perhaps open onto the universal. Which is something that I couldn't do before, when I was trying to write in some universal way.

ACKNOWLEDGMENTS

So many helped bring this work to life. First and foremost, Chris Ashley and Gabe Green and everyone at La Jolla Playhouse, where this play first saw the light of day. Paige Evans and Andre Bishop and the amazing staff of LCT3 / Lincoln Center Theater, where it found its finished form. Judy Clain, Terry Adams, Nicole Dewey, and the rest of Little, Brown and Co., for this edition. My indispensable agents Chris Till and Donna Bagdasarian. And of course, Marc Glick.

A play is a collaboration with so many artists. Kimberly Senior, my director from day one. Bernie White, ever Afzal. The amazing design teams in La Jolla and New York: Jack Magaw, Jill BC Du Boff, Elisa Benzoni, Jaymi Lee Smith, Emily Rebholz, Japhy Weideman. Casting directors Sharon Bialy and Gohar Gazazyan on the West Coast and Daniel Swee on the East Coast. And the wonderful actors who participated at every stage of this process: Greg Keller, Nadine Malouf, Tala Ashe, Meera Rohit Kumbhani, Karen David, Dieterich Gray, Sheila Vand, Monika Jolly, Jolly Abraham, Ryan O'Nan, Faran Tahir, Stephen Plunkett, Roxanna Hope, Demosthenes Chrysan, and Anitha Gandhi.

I benefited from the insights of so many: Don Shaw, Steve Klein, Ami Dayan, Poorna Jagannathan, Dan Hancock, Shazad

Akhtar, Shirley Fishman, Gaye Taylor Upchurch, Eric Rosen at Kansas City Rep, Seth Gordon at The Rep of St. Louis, Polly Carl, Natasha Sinha, Michael Pollard, Madani Younis at the Bush Theatre in London, Amanda Watkins at the Araca Group, Stuart Rosenthal, and Jerry Patch and Annie MacRae at MTC.

Finally, I want to acknowledge the support of Ritu Sahai-Mittal and Manish Mittal, as well as the Blanche and Irving Laurie Foundation.

ABOUT THE AUTHOR

AYAD AKHTAR is a screenwriter, playwright, actor, and novelist. He was nominated for a 2006 Independent Spirit Award for best screenplay for the film *The War Within*. His plays include *Disgraced*, produced at New York's Lincoln Center Theater in 2012 and recipient of the 2013 Pulitzer Prize for Drama. He lives in New York City.

. . . AND HIS NOVEL

American Dervish was hailed by *People* as "a particularly fresh and touching coming-of-age story." Following is an excerpt from the book's opening pages.

Mina

Long before I knew Mina, I knew her story.

It was a tale Mother told so many times: How her best friend, gifted and gorgeous—something of a genius, as Mother saw it—had been frustrated at every turn, her development derailed by the small-mindedness of her family, her robust will checked by a culture that made no place for a woman. I heard about the grades Mina skipped and the classes she topped, though always somewhat to the chagrin of parents more concerned with her eventual nuptials than her report card. I heard about all the boys who loved her, and how—when she was twelve—she, too, fell in love, only to have her nose broken by her father's fist when he found a note from her sweetheart tucked into her math book. I heard about her nervous breakdowns and her troubles with food and, of course, about the trove of poems her mother set alight in the living room fireplace one night during an argument about whether or not Mina would be allowed to go to college to become a writer.

Perhaps it was that I heard it all so often without knowing the woman myself, but for the longest time, Mina Ali and her gifts and travails were like the persistent smell of curry in our halls and our rooms: an ever-presence in my life of which I made little note.

And then, one summer afternoon when I was eight, I saw a picture of her. As Mother unfolded Mina's latest letter from Pakistan, a palm-sized color glossy tumbled out. "That's your auntie Mina, *kurban,*" Mother said as I picked it up. "Look how beautiful she is."

Beautiful, indeed.

The picture showed a striking woman sitting on a wicker chair before a background of green leaves and orange flowers. Most of her perfectly black hair was covered with a pale pink scarf, and both her hair and scarf framed an utterly arresting face: cheekbones highly drawn—gently accentuated with a touch of blush—oval eyes, and a small, pointed nose perched above a pair of ample lips. Her features defined a perfect harmony, promising something sheltering, something tender, but not only. For there was an intensity in her eyes that belied this intimation of maternal comfort, or at least complicated it: those eyes were black and filled with piercing light, as if her vision had long been sharpened against the grindstone of some nameless inner pain. And though she was smiling, her smile was more one concealed than offered and, like her eyes, hinted at something mysterious and elusive, something you wanted to know.

Mother posted the photo on our refrigerator door, pinned in place by the same rainbow-shaped finger magnets that also affixed my school lunch menu. (This was the menu Mother consulted each night before school to see if pork was being served the following day—and if, therefore, I'd be needing a bag lunch—and which I consulted each school morning hoping to find my favorite, beef lasagna, listed among the day's offerings.) For two years, then, barely a day went by without at least a casual glance at that photograph of Mina. And there were more than a few occasions when, finishing my glass of morning milk, or munching on string cheese after school, I lingered over it, staring at her likeness as I sometimes did at the surface of the pond at Worth Park on summer afternoons: doing my best to catch a glimpse of what was hidden in the depths.

It was a remarkable photograph, and—as I was to discover from Mina herself a couple of years later—it had an equally remarkable history. Mina's parents, counting on their daughter's beauty to attract a lucrative match, brought in a fashion photographer to take pictures of her, and the photo in question was the one that would make its way—through a matchmaker—into the hands of Hamed Suhail, the only son of a wealthy Karachi family.

Hamed fell in love with Mina the moment he saw it.

The Suhails showed up at the Ali home a week and a half later, and by the end of their meeting, the fathers had shaken hands on their children's betrothal. Mother always claimed that Mina didn't dislike Hamed, and that Mina always said she could have found happiness with him. If not for Irshad, Hamed's mother.

After the wedding, Mina moved south to Karachi to live with her in-laws, and the problems between mother-in-law and daughter-in-law began the first night Mina was there. Irshad came into her bedroom holding a string of plump, pomegranate-colored stones, a garnet necklace and family heirloom which— Irshad explained—had been handed down from mother to daughter for five generations. Herself daughterless, Irshad had always imagined she would bestow these, the only family jewels, on the wife of her only son someday.

"Try it on," Irshad urged, warmly.

Mina did. And as they both stared into the mirror, Mina couldn't help but notice the silvery thinning of Irshad's eyes. She recognized the envy.

"You shouldn't, *Ammi*," Mina said, pulling the stones from her neck.

"I shouldn't what?"

"I don't know...I mean, it's so beautiful...are you sure you want to give it to me?"

"I'm not giving it to you *yet*," Irshad replied, abruptly. "I just wanted to see how it looked."

Bruised by Irshad's sudden shift, Mina handed the necklace back to her mother-in-law. Irshad took it and, without another word, walked out of the room.

So Irshad's enmity began. First came the snide comments offered under her breath, or in passing: about how headstrong the "new girl" was; how she ate hunched over her plate like a servant; or how, as Irshad put it, Mina looked like a "mouse." Soon to follow were changes to the household routine intended to make Mina's life more difficult: servants sent up to clean Mina's room when she was still asleep; the expunging from the family menu of the foods Mina most enjoyed; the continued flurry of mean-spirited remarks, though now no longer offered sotto voce. Mina did all she could to appease and placate her mother-in-law. But this only stoked Irshad's suspicions. For as Mina tried to ply Irshad with submissiveness, the elder woman felt the change of tack, and read it as evidence of a cunning nature. Irshad now started rumors about her daughter-in-law's "wandering eyes" and "thieving hands." She warned her son to keep Mina away from the male staff, and warned her staff to keep their valuables

under lock and key. (Neither Hamed nor his father—both terrified of Irshad—did anything to address the growing conflict.)
And when the pleasure of verbal abuse wore thin, Irshad resorted
to the physical. Now she slapped Mina, for leaving her dirty
clothes strewn around her bedroom, or talking out of turn in
front of guests. On one occasion, hearing an insult in a comment
Mina made about dinner not being as spicy as usual, Irshad
grabbed her daughter-in-law by the hair and dragged her from
the dinner table to throw her out into the hallway.

Fourteen months into this growing nightmare, Mina con-
ceived. To escape the abuse and bring her pregnancy to term in
peace, she returned north to her family home, in the Punjab.
There, three weeks early, unaccompanied by her husband—who
would not join her for fear of suffering his mother's wrath—Mina
gave birth to a boy. And as she lay in the hospital bed exhausted
from her daylong labor, a man in a long dark coat appeared at the
doorway just moments after her mother left the room to fetch a
cup of tea from the canteen. He stepped inside, inquiring if she
was Amina Suhail née Ali.

"I am," Mina replied.

The man approached her bedside, an envelope in hand. "Your
husband has divorced you. Enclosed are the papers that make
this divorce official. He has written in his own hand—you will
recognize the writing—that he divorces you, he divorces you,
and he divorces you. As you well know, Mrs. Suhail—I mean,
Ms. Ali—this is what the law requires." He laid the envelope
across her belly, gently. "You have just given birth to Hamed
Suhail's son. He has chosen the name Imran for the boy. Imran
will stay with you until the age of seven, at which point
Mr. Hamed Suhail has the right to full, undisputed custody."

The lawyer took a step back, but he wasn't finished. Mina squinted at him in disbelief. "All that I have shared with you is in accordance with the law as it stands, this date of June 15, 1976, in the land of Pakistan, and you are entitled to a custody trial by law, but I would advise you to understand, Mrs. Suhail—I mean, Ms. Ali—that any fight will be a useless one for you, and will simply cost your family resources it does not have."

Then the lawyer turned and walked out.

Mina cried for days and nights and weeks to follow. Yet, devastated as she was by Hamed's brutality—and terrified by his menacing promise to take her son away someday—when she stared down into her infant's eyes, she nevertheless cooed to him with the name that her now-ex-husband had chosen without her:

She called the boy Imran.